VACATION PEOPLE

Cheri Ritz

About the Author

Cheri Ritz loves a good romance novel so much that she decided to write one of her own! She enjoys attending her sons' many activities, volunteering with a local LGBT film festival, and spending cozy weekends marathoning TV shows. She lives in a suburb of Pittsburgh, Pennsylvania with her girlfriend, three sons, and the sweetest cat in the world.

VACATION PEOPLE

Cheri Ritz

BELLA
B O O K S
2020

Bella Books, Inc.
P.O. Box 10543
Tallahassee, FL 32302

Printed in the United States of America on acid-free paper.

First Bella Books Edition 2020

Editor: Ann Roberts
Cover Designer: Judith Fellows

ISBN: 978-1-64247-103-8

Acknowledgments

Thanks first and foremost to the good people at Bella Books who have been so supportive and all around wonderful to work with. I'm honored to be counted among their authors.

A great big thanks to Ann Roberts, my editor, who whipped this story into shape with the perfect combination of toughness and kindness. The book wouldn't be what it is today without all I learned working with her.

Thank you to Jaime who inspires me every day. Her encouragement and wit never fail, and I couldn't do what I do if she wasn't by my side.

And thanks to my boys for reminding me to never give up on dreams, and showing me that being true to yourself never goes out of style.

For Jaime
My real life Happily Ever After

CHAPTER ONE

Penny Rothmoor liked things to be in order. As she surveyed the hustle and bustle around her, she straightened her back and then straightened the lapels on her jacket. She loved being a part of her family's casino in her role as Operations Manager. This was where she belonged: next in line to head up the Rothmoor Towers Casino dynasty.

"I think this constitutes abuse. This is like the tenth hand in a row I've lost. What are you trying to do to me, Rothmoor?"

"Ha, ha." Penny snapped out of her reverie in time to cut off her best friend's grumbling. To smooth things over with the other patrons she added, "Comedian Mara Antonini everybody. Catch her act tonight at the Laffmoor Comedy Club upstairs."

Mara scooped up her last few chips and slid off her perch. "Sorry, I had to say something. You had that intense 'I'm a boss' look you get sometimes. I was just trying to lighten the mood."

"There's nothing wrong with taking pride in one's work." Penny stuck out her chin defiantly.

"Loving your job is one thing, but acting like a robot is a whole other thing." To emphasize her point Mara broke out in a jerky stiff-armed dance, but just as suddenly she sobered up and her mouth fixed into a frown. "Don't turn around. Bryce just walked into the casino."

"What the hell is he doing here?" Penny's fingers grasped the green felt on the edge of the blackjack table. After the way her ex had destroyed their relationship and humiliated her in the process, she couldn't stand the thought of even looking at him.

"Oh man, he's heading this way," Mara confirmed.

"Penny, I need to talk to you," Bryce announced in his deep dopey voice, making her back go as stiff as the drink she would need after this confrontation.

Penny quickly sized up the situation as she met him with a glare. While this was probably a conversation they should have in private, the chances of her dragging Bryce's solid six-foot-four frame out of the area without causing a scene were slim. She had to keep her cool, act professional, and solve the problem with a quick exchange of words. "You have a lot of fucking nerve showing your face in this casino. I have nothing else to say to you."

Bryce shrugged his beefy shoulders. "Your phone isn't working and I think I left some stuff in our…your suite. I want it back."

Her phone wasn't working because she'd changed her number shortly after their breakup. She was totally done with Bryce Kellar. "I assure you I'm not going to keep any of your action figure collectibles or some ratty old Beta Nu T-shirt. Should I unearth one of them in my suite, I'll return it immediately. Please leave and don't come back to the Rothmoor ever again."

"You're pissed because I quit my job here."

"You went to work for a competitor and took a decent chunk of the casino's security staff with you."

"I had to do something," he scowled. "I have a life here now. I moved to Las Vegas to be with you and then you became completely emotionally unavailable."

"Emotionally unavailable?" Penny curled her hand around a stack of poker chips on the table beside her. Her jaw clenched in anger the same way it had the afternoon she returned to her suite midshift to find Bryce in bed with one of the dancers from the Rothmoor Revue. She struggled to keep her voice down and her temper in control. "You cheated on me...*again.*" To her horror she watched as the fistful of chips bounced off Bryce's broad chest and rained down onto the casino floor at her feet. She hadn't even realized she'd thrown them, but the gasps of the patrons seated around the blackjack table confirmed that the incident hadn't gone unnoticed by others.

Bryce was still gaping at her in surprise when Penny felt her father's strong, calming hand on her shoulder.

"Mr. Kellar, I'm afraid I have to ask you to leave the casino." Her father's voice was firm but not unkind as he continued, "Penny, please go to the boardroom. I'll meet you there momentarily."

Penny paced the length of the boardroom in front of the floor-to-ceiling windows. Not even the breathtaking view of the glittering casinos and flashing neon signs of Las Vegas, the city she grew up in and loved, could make her stomach unclench after the blow she had just been dealt.

She glared at Timothy in his neat, classic-fit, tailored suit. "I don't need time off. I can separate my work and personal life just fine." She held her head up high and swallowed hard against the panic rising in her throat. She had always been proud to be a part of the success of the family business, and her job was everything to her. An uncomfortable tingle traveled up her neck and into her cheeks. It hurt that her boss was ordering her to take time off work. The fact that her boss was also her father made it feel like the ultimate betrayal. "Why the hell isn't my father standing up for me?"

"This *is* your father standing up for you." Timothy smirked at her mention of family ties, the one advantage at the casino he could never take from her. He leaned forward with both hands on the conference table, causing his bright red tie to swing limply in front of him. "Your *fiancé* left his position as head of security at the Rothmoor and took half of our security staff with him. Bryce Kellar left the Rothmoor's employ because you broke things off with him. Revenge for being dumped. Your reputation was already on shaky ground for bringing him on board here in the first place, but then you went and made a scene on the casino floor today. It's like you've totally snapped. Your father is worried about you."

God, Timothy was a snotty bitch when he wanted to be. A weight settled on her heart at the mention of her love lost. She and Bryce had been together off and on since they were in college nearly ten years ago. During the off times she had dated other guys and girls, but somehow she always ended up giving Bryce one more chance. This last attempt with Bryce had felt like the real deal. Sadly, being older and wiser didn't make them any more able to make their relationship work this time either. She searched Timothy's face, hoping to see even the faintest glimmer of understanding in his eyes or a hint of humanity, but he held true to form. *Cold ass, stab you in the back, spit on your neck snake.* Would it seriously kill him to show a little compassion for her situation?

"We both ended our relationship. It was a mutual decision." Penny's shoulders tensed. She didn't need to explain herself. It was none of his business. It was none of *anyone's* business. She clenched her jaw as she struggled to keep her emotions in check in front of Timothy. She didn't need to *snap* again. "Don't paint me as the bad guy here."

"I'm not painting you as anything." Timothy straightened his posture, pushing at his jacket to shove his hands in his pants pockets—the picture-perfect combination of smooth professionalism and smarmy narcissism. Of all the people in his employ, why did her father have to choose Timothy to deliver the news? Of course none of it was Timothy's fault. He was just the messenger, but he was quickly becoming the target of Penny's wrath at the indignity of the situation, especially since he seemed to relish the duty of delivering it. "This has nothing to do with how I see you and your breakup with Bryce." His voice took on a haughty, staccato edge that made Penny cringe.

"It's your father's belief that right now the best thing for you to do is lie low and let this all blow over. Take some time off. You're still getting paid, so just relax and enjoy it. In a couple weeks when things have quieted down and returned to normal, we'll bring you back."

Relax and enjoy it? A couple weeks? Penny's blood boiled at Timothy's cool, calm tone. He wasn't the one who would be stuck jobless, lost and useless, watching reruns of *Family Feud* and eating leftover takeout because there was no point in getting dressed and leaving the suite. He would be at the Rothmoor, probably doing her job as Operations Manager and gaining the upper hand on her in the business while she sat idly by. "You'll bring me back when things *return to normal?* Are you fucking with me?"

"No, Miss Rothmoor." Timothy's voice took on a precise crispness that indicated he was out of patience with her. She was more than familiar with the tone. "I assure you that I am in no way *fucking* with you. This is your father's final decision. You are officially off duty as soon as you deliver those to the front desk." He gestured lazily at three brown boxes piled on the opposite end of the table before spinning on his Brooks Brothers wingtips and leaving her speechless and temporarily jobless in the conference room.

Delivering boxes to the front desk. There was no doubt in her mind that he had thrown that task in purely as a kick to her gut while she was down.

The elevator dinged cheerfully in the hallway, reminding her that life in the casino was going on without her already. She drifted back to the tall windows that showcased the Vegas skyline. In the dusky shades of early evening, the glow of neon lights began to come alive. Sparkling and shining, they beckoned gamblers to come out and play. Come take a chance. Her gaze ran down the strip, following a tiny car on the street below as it passed so many favorite places in her hometown. She waited for the surge of energy the view usually inspired in her, but this time she came up empty. She sighed and turned her back to the window, focusing instead on the portrait of her great-grandfather that hung above the massive conference table. From his perch on the wall, it seemed like he still kept an eye on what went on at the casino he built so many years ago.

She'd facilitated a hundred meetings in that conference room as Lead Floor Manager at the Rothmoor and now she was being asked to stay away. Her scalp prickled with shame. What would her great-grandfather think about that? From what Timothy had said, she had really let her father down with the scene she'd made in the casino. What if he decided she was no longer needed? What if she was replaceable? She dismissed the thought as preposterous even as it crossed her mind. She was *damn good* at what she did. *But still…*

What would she do to fill her days for the next couple weeks? Ironically, she now had time to plan that wedding that she and Bryce had just called off. She rubbed at her temples in an attempt to soothe the tension throbbing there. Truth be told, she was already missing her job much more than she missed him.

She sucked in her breath and fought the tears prickling at her eyes. She still had to walk out of the office suite, and she sure as hell wasn't going to do it a sobbing mess. She clicked on her phone and stabbed at the keypad. She needed a plan, even if it were just for the immediate future. She needed to get out of the casino.

Fortunately, her best friend Mara picked up on the first ring. "Blue Balls Deli. No one beats our meat!"

"Mara, I…" she choked out. She would not cry. Not at work.

"Hey, are you okay?" Mara's tone shifted to soft and concerned, despite the rowdy voices in the background on her end. "I can't talk for long here."

"I know, I know." Penny blinked back the tears still threatening to fall. Mara Antonini wasn't just her best friend, she was also the headliner at the Rothmoor's comedy club. "You have a show starting in like, minutes. I know that. I was being stupid. I'm looking for someone to get a drink or ten with. I wasn't thinking."

"Whoa, back it up." Just the sound of Mara's voice was a comfort. "Why aren't you working? And why are you drinking? Penny, what the hell is going on?"

"I've been..." What was the word for her situation? Suspended? Laid off? "I've been asked to take a break from work."

"What? Why? That doesn't make any sense." Mara sounded as stunned as Penny felt.

"Because of the whole thing with Bryce today. I don't want to talk about it. I want to drink." She sniffled. "Can you meet me after your show?"

"I can—" Mara began hesitantly. "But aren't you forgetting something?"

Penny swiped a thumb under each of her eyes. She still needed to pull it together before she could leave the conference room. She took another deep breath to steady herself. "No, I know you have two shows tonight."

"I was referring to your dinner date with that old friend of your mom's." Mara's voice took on the sound of worry. "Honey, it's not like you to forget stuff like that. You're really shaken up, aren't you?"

Dinner with Lauren Hansen. Fuck. Penny had totally forgotten. She didn't even know the woman, but she had reached out after hearing Penny's mother had passed last year. "Ugh. Yeah, you could say that. I don't know what the hell I'm doing right now." She shook her head in an attempt to clear it. "Okay, I'll go to dinner with Lauren, get that over with, and be at Game of Flats by nine thirty. Text the other girls and tell them to meet me."

"You got it," Mara confirmed. "And you try to relax. We'll get this all figured out. Gotta run. See you tonight." She clicked off the call.

Taking control of the moment had given Penny the boost she needed to get out of the conference room without completely falling apart. She slipped her phone into her pocket, threw her shoulders back, and stuck her chin out, summoning the old, "fake it 'til you make it" mindset of her younger years. She would deliver the boxes to the front desk, go to her suite for a change of clothes, meet Lauren for dinner, and then drown her sorrows at Game of Flats with her friends. All she had to do was stick to the plan and everything would be okay.

CHAPTER TWO

Lauren Hansen stood all alone by the baggage carousel. She hitched her purse up on her shoulder and hummed *We Got The Beat*, the last song she had listened to on the plane. She tapped her foot and surveyed the crowd of fellow travelers around her. Most of them seemed to be paired up, if not part of a group. With a sigh she returned her gaze to the parade of bags. The trip was not going at all as she had imagined it when she'd sat at her computer months ago looking at photos of sunny resorts and happy couples, but she was doing her best to forge on just the same. Back then she was planning a trip for two. As she stood watching other people's luggage file by on the moving belt, she was a solo act. If there was one thing she had learned in her fifty years on this Earth, it was that plans were always subject to change.

When she had booked the trip, she had been part of a couple celebrating their ten-year anniversary and marking the occasion with a trip to the Waverly Winds Resort on the island of Hawaii. That was before Carolyn betrayed her. Before Carolyn announced she didn't *want them* anymore. Before Carolyn walked out on her and their life together. Before Lauren was alone.

Suddenly, taking the trip by herself seemed like a very stupid idea.

She *could* just grab her bag, march herself to the counter, and book a flight back home to Chicago. She had a gallery showing for her photographs right after she was scheduled to get back from the vacation anyway. She could skip the trip and spend the time preparing, over preparing, really, since everything was already lined up and set to go. Of course, Penny Rothmoor was expecting her for dinner. She *could* just cancel on that as well. Hell, she didn't even know the woman.

Lauren's rust orange suitcase slid out of the chute and onto the belt, one bright spot in a sea of black bags. She snapped back to reality. She needed to get outside. She would be able to think more clearly in the fresh air.

Ten minutes later she was standing on the curb, but she was in no real hurry to hail a cab. She squinted against the brightness of the sun, but the heat on her face had a soothing effect. Her shoulders relaxed as a layer of tension melted away. May weather in Las Vegas was a whole different ballgame than May weather in Chicago. She had heard it was the month when the temperature there took a turn from comfortable spring to the blazing hot heat of summer. The scorching sun above was most certainly a testament to that. Lauren had left behind overcast skies and a chilly morning back home. She had shoved her Anne Klein tweed topper jacket into her carry-on when her flight had landed. She doubted she would need it for the remainder of her trip.

A family of travelers spilled out of the airport and rushed toward a waiting van by the curb. Couples climbed into cabs, anxious to reach their next destination. A group of boisterous golf buddies loaded their suitcases and club bags into the back of a black town car.

All the while Lauren stood by herself. She took a deep breath of the warm Las Vegas air. *Should I stay or should I go?*

Her brain had moved on to another song. The sun on her face felt damn good, and she allowed a few more bars of the song to run through her head while she stood there on the sidewalk considering her next move. The choice really was hers.

As if on cue, her phone rang, announcing her assistant James was trying to reach her. Lauren clicked on the call but didn't get in a word before James started in on her. "You were supposed to call me as soon as you landed. Is everything okay? You had me worried sick. Are you in Vegas? Is it true what they say about the dry heat? I hope you packed your moisturizer. I don't know if my skin could take it." He finally paused to take a breath.

"I'm fine, James, and it's a glorious day here in Nevada." She couldn't resist a little poke at him. "I was just wondering if this vacation was a good idea. Do you think I should just scrap it and come back home?"

"What? You better be joking," he scolded. "You need this vacation. You *deserve* it. You've been working yourself into the ground. No. You *will* vacation and come back to me relaxed and rejuvenated, just in time for opening night."

"You're bossy today. It makes me miss you." She laughed at James's chattering and gave a stiff nod to the airport security officer walking the length of the loading area.

"Well, stop missing me and start vacationing. I mean it. We've talked this through a million times. There's nothing to be done here before the show opens, and I don't need you overthinking and overstressing and messing with perfection. That kind of thing is very bad for the complexion. Get your ass directly to Hawaii. You're on vacation."

Hearing James's voice had given her the boost she needed to push forward with the original plan. He was right, of course. She was likely to drive him mad if she was just hanging around in Chicago, second-guessing everything they had set in place for the show. She pulled a deep breath of warm air into her lungs and boosted her bag on her shoulder. Onward and upward it would be. She put her hand in the air to hail a taxi as she responded to her assistant's firm instruction. "I guess I have no choice. I'm on vacation."

CHAPTER THREE

Penny scooped the pile of boxes into her arms. She could see over the top, and they weren't heavy, but they were awkward in her grasp. With a deep sigh, she balanced them against her chest and wedged herself through the door of the conference room into the hallway.

As if the whole mandatory vacation thing wasn't shameful enough, being sent off with this final, lowly task was a big kick in the ass. All the way down to the front desk too. She would be bumbling through the middle of the lobby with the doomed boxes stacked in her arms. If one toppled off in front of everybody, she would feel like a fool. She could have gotten a dolly from maintenance and wheeled the pile down, but that would have just stretched the task out longer. All she wanted to do now was be done. Damn Timothy! She wouldn't miss working with him one bit while she was off.

She stepped out of the elevator and into the buzz of action that was a typical Friday afternoon at the Rothmoor. She circumvented the queue of guests checking in, being extra careful to avoid the tourists milling around gawking at the impossibly high ceiling and Old Hollywood gilded décor. Bobbing and weaving through the crowd of gamblers heading straight to the casino floor to dance with lady luck, she made her way toward the front desk. All she needed to do was deposit the boxes with the smiling face on duty there and she was free. Well, if she put a happy spin on being asked to leave her job temporarily and called it freedom. But less than twenty steps away from delivering the boxes to their destination without incident, someone bumped into her from behind, startling her just enough to cause her to lose her footing.

The offending tourist called out an apology to her as he continued on his way, but she barely heard it. In her effort to keep herself upright, Penny jostled the boxes in her arms and to her horror, she felt herself losing her hold on them. All she could do was watch as they tumbled to the floor. Stress and frustration from the events of the afternoon bubbled up inside of her. A shudder rippled through her shoulders and she pressed her eyelids shut tight as she dropped to her knees to gather the packages. She had made it that far through the disaster of a day without crying, and she wasn't going to start now. "Son of a fucking—"

"Do you need a hand?"

The heat already building in Penny's cheeks from her embarrassing case of the dropsies ratcheted up a notch. Her mini-meltdown had been overheard. So much for her reputation as an upstanding professional. It had pretty much been blown to hell in one damn day. She looked up to decline the stranger's offer, but the words caught in her throat as she saw the beautiful woman gazing down at her.

Amusement flashed in the woman's olive green eyes and a smile played at her lips, a striking contrast to the strict bun her auburn hair was fixed in. Her long jewel-tone print skirt swirled around her legs like flower petals opening to blossom as she bent down to assist. "Let me help, Penny."

Surprise caused Penny's breath to hitch again as the woman called her by name. She studied her face carefully as the brunette reached for a box. Soft wisps of hair that had fallen from her bun framed a tanned face that had a smooth complexion except for joyful laugh lines at the corners of her kind eyes. The woman was a Grade-A knockout, but it was her bright open smile that held Penny's attention and pinged in her mind as a familiar sight. A warmth stirred within her—a memory of happiness and comfort and her mother's voice. As she rose again with two of the boxes in her arms, it struck her. She recalled the photograph of her mother and this woman, two grinning kids arm in arm, mugging for the camera.

"You're Lauren Hansen."

"Yes, I am." She stood posed with one of Penny's stray boxes hitched up on her hip. A smirk crossed her lips and her cheeks appled. "I wasn't sure you would recognize me."

"I remember you from a picture my mother used to have framed on her vanity. And, of course, from your website." The burn in Penny's cheeks traveled down her neck. First she lost her cool in the middle of the lobby. Second, she did so in the presence of her mother's oldest friend, who also happened to be gorgeous, and finally, she flat-out admitted that she had creeped her online.

"Oh my God. Are we supposed to be meeting now? I thought we were doing dinner." It suddenly occurred to her that maybe she had been mistaken about the time she and Lauren were supposed to meet. After all, Lauren was there in the lobby of the Rothmoor, still smiling kindly in spite of Penny's stumbling, bumbling, and embarrassing confessions of cyberstalking.

"Relax." Lauren shifted the box on her hip and rested her free hand on Penny's shoulder. "I'm early. I figured I would stroll around and take in the sights at the Rothmoor until it was time for us to meet. I'm not really much of a gambler, but I'm a huge fan of people watching. I'll be fine. A place like this offers endless possibilities for it."

I can't let her do that! This is one of my mom's dearest friends. Penny needed to get herself together and turn on her manners and charm. She drew in a deep breath and stuck her chest out. She fixed a smile on her face that wouldn't betray the fact that she was dying on the inside over the whole work thing. She had a duty to her family that went beyond her job at the casino. That duty included honoring her mother in any way possible, even playing the hostess with the mostest. "Why don't you come up to my suite? I'll make us drinks, get changed for dinner, and we can be on our way. Do you like brandy?"

"I don't want to impose."

"Don't be ridiculous. I mix a mean sidecar, and besides, hanging out in my suite beats the heck out of watching tourists pump quarters into slot machines. Trust me. I do both regularly, so I know."

Lauren took a sip of her sidecar and paced the length of Penny's living room. The furniture was stylish and new, but the walls were surprisingly bare. She wrinkled her nose at the only knickknack propped on the mantle—some weird, clown mask thing. It certainly didn't attest much to Penny's sense of style. Penny looked so much like her mother, but Shelly would have had a thing or two to say about the décor in this suite, and it wouldn't have been positive.

Lauren smiled fondly at the thought of Shelly and some of her wild outfits and her sense of style from when they were young—bright, bold prints often worn mishmashed together, ripped denim jeans and jackets, and lord, the hats. The 80s truly were *totally awesome*. Shelly couldn't have possibly had a hand in decorating her daughter's suite—the stark white walls, the lack of art. Hell, even the throw pillows on the couch were a bland black and white. Maybe it had to do with some sort of rebellious nature in Penny. She chose the opposite of what her mother would have opted for completely out of spite, as daughters sometimes did.

Lauren swished the brandy in her mouth before swallowing, allowing it to tingle on her tongue and the inside of her cheeks. Shelly might not have remained the colorful, bright-print girl she was when they were younger, once she grew up and became Michelle Rothmoor. For all Lauren knew, those years of being a Rothmoor could have completely changed her style. Tamed it.

Lauren's eyes prickled with threatening tears at the regret and guilt she felt for letting their friendship fade over the years. She hadn't even known Shelly was sick. She had come back from a trip to Italy to hear of her friend's passing. James had seen something about the Rothmoor family on the Internet and recalled the wife of the casino owner had been a friend of hers. She had missed the funeral while she was out of the country.

She wasn't even sure when she'd last spoken to Shelly. She had sent a gift when Penny was born, but that was thirty-two years ago. The women still talked on the phone regularly back then. Then they both got deeper and deeper into their own lives. Shelly raised her child and Lauren established her art career. *I'll call next week* turned into next month, then next year. Before she knew it, decades had gone by. When Lauren had learned her best friend from all those years ago had lost her battle with cancer, she thought the least she could do was reach out to Penny and offer her condolences. It was her only hope for closure with a friend she had held so dear for so long, despite the distance between them.

"I'm almost ready," Penny called from her bedroom.

"Take your time. I'm just…admiring your suite."

"You mean wondering why the place looks so damn empty." Penny laughed as she set her glass on a side table and took a moment to fasten her earring in place. "I'm sorry. It's not usually like this. I'm between décors." Her expression suddenly clouded with sadness. "I'm in between lots of things it seems. Want another drink?"

The shift in Penny's mood wasn't lost on Lauren. Poor girl, she sounded like she needed someone to talk to. Lauren had the whole night in Vegas ahead of her with no plans other than her dinner with Penny. If Shelly's daughter needed an ear and a shoulder to cry on, Lauren would be that person. She owed Shelly that much. She sucked the last of the liquid out of her own glass before holding it out in front of her. "Sure, I'll take another."

By the time the women were eating dinner in the corner booth in Daisy Jane's, the Rothmoor Casino's steakhouse, Penny had shared with Lauren most of the epic tale of her breakup with Bryce and its fallout. She was surprised by the relief she felt simply by speaking what was on her mind out loud, and she appreciated Lauren's letting her do it.

"So, your ex-fiancé cheated on you then left his position as head of security here at the Rothmoor and took a new job at a rival casino?" Lauren shook her head sympathetically. "That's low."

Penny picked at the edge of the linen napkin in her lap. "The worst part is that he took the bulk of our security staff with him. We had to bring in contractors to fill in while we searched for new staff. That's the thing that made my father angry. Of course, I imagine he's not thrilled with the part where I lost my temper and made a scene in the middle of the casino either."

"I'm so sorry. I know this can't be easy for you." Lauren took a sip of her water. She had finished the second sidecar back in the room, but once they got to the restaurant she had gone alcohol free. "I only met your father one time, when your mother first met him, but I've read about his business success over the years. I'm sure this is only a minor setback for the casino. Give it a little time to blow over."

"You were with my mom when she met my father? I didn't know that."

"Oh, yes." Lauren smiled and leaned back against the high back of the booth. She raised one eyebrow mysteriously as if she were about to reveal top-secret information. It worked. Penny leaned closer, intrigued by the tease. "Your mom and I came here the summer after she graduated from high school with fake IDs, big party dreams, and even bigger hair."

Penny bit the inside of her cheek to hold in a giggle at the thought of her mom as a rebellious teen. It was a far cry from the proper woman who was always dressed to the nines and served on the boards of at least a dozen charities over the years. In spite of her effort, her amusement must have shown on her face.

"I know, I know. It was a different time. Fake IDs were easier to pull off back in the day. And we were very young and *very* silly. It was nineteen eighty-six and I was only sixteen that summer."

Lauren's eyes sparkled with some of that mischief left over from her younger days. "Our big eighties hair and the eye shadow made us look older. Anyway, Shelly met your father while we were here in town, and that was it. She was in love. I had to go back home after our vacation was over and finish up high school, but not your mom. She never looked back."

"My mom told me about you two being friends when you were in school, but not the part about how she came here to Vegas with you." Penny couldn't imagine her mother ever confessing to her about using a fake ID, but knowing that detail about her younger years was a comfort somehow. Lauren was giving her a true gift by sharing these small things. She didn't know much about her mother's life pre-Vegas. It was as if her life only really began once she got married. "My mom never really talked about anything that happened before she lived here."

Lauren set her knife and fork on her plate in the five o'clock position indicating she was finished with her meal. She pressed her lips together as if choosing her words carefully. "Well, her life back in Illinois wasn't all that great. She had lost her own mother when she was very young, as I'm sure you know. Her father was a hard-working man and did the best he could raising her, but by the time we were in high school, he was a pretty hard drinker. He kept to himself—didn't do anything to hurt her or anything like that. But your mom was on her own most of the time. I always knew she was just biding her time until she could get the hell out of Dodge. Meeting your father and falling in love with him was a real fairytale ending for her. I missed her after I left her in Las Vegas, but I was happy for her."

"We should all be so lucky." Penny held up her glass in a toast. She was filled with warmth from both the alcohol and the joy of making a new friend. "To fairytale endings for all of us."

Sadness briefly flashed in Lauren's eyes, but then she raised her glass as well. "Hear, hear." Her expression shifted completely again as she seemed to catch sight of something just past their table out of Penny's line of vision. "Speak of the devil, here comes your father now."

Penny swallowed her mouthful of Malbec hard. She had enjoyed the respite from thinking about what had happened in the boardroom earlier in the day while Lauren had entertained her with stories of her mother, but reality was crashing back in. The fact was, she had acted completely unprofessionally in the casino earlier and she deserved the consequences her father had passed down. Shame opened the door for anxiety to come on in and her stomach clenched with nerves. She needed to apologize for her behavior, but she wasn't ready to face her father yet, not by a long shot. As he continued walking in their direction, she slouched down in her seat, pressed her back against the leather booth, and lowered her voice. "Did he see me? Do you think he saw me?"

Lauren hushed her voice conspiratorially as she kept her eye on the situation. "I don't think so. I'm guessing you don't want me to wave hello to him."

"I'm still so hurt, and angry, and embarrassed enough that I've been furloughed. I don't need to cry in the middle of the Daisy Jane over it as well." She skirted the truth. "Can we just get out of here?"

Lauren's eyebrows shot up in alarm as she considered the proposition, but then she gave a stiff nod as if she had resolved to take charge of the situation. "Okay. Grab a hold of your purse and be ready to scoot out of this booth on my signal. Don't hesitate, don't look back. Scurry on out front and I'll meet you there shortly after."

Penny drained the last of her wine and slipped her hand through the thin strap of her clutch. What a damn day. Ducking out of the steakhouse in an effort to run away from her father/boss was really the topper. She stared intently at Lauren, who watched Penny's father. The moment Lauren flicked her wrist toward the entrance, Penny put her head down and made a beeline for the exit as instructed. Her heart was still pounding in her chest minutes later when Lauren finally emerged from the restaurant. Her long stride was calm and confident, quite the contrast to Penny's own hurried and clumsy departure from the Daisy Jane. Laughter bubbled up inside of her as the adrenaline rush took a turn and the absurdity of her childish behavior kicked in, but Lauren simply linked their arms and they sauntered lazily away from the steakhouse as if nothing had happened.

"Thank you for going along with that." Penny grinned when her breathing finally slowed to a normal rate. "I don't know why my sense of fight or flight kicked in. I guess I'm still processing everything that happened today."

"You're welcome. I'm happy to help." Lauren gave her arm a little squeeze and bumped their shoulders together, a mini hug that for some reason made Penny's heart rate speed up again, but this time in a very different way.

"You were a real star back there. Usually the only person I get into wacky situations with is my best friend, Mara." Penny's hand flew up to cover her mouth as she gasped at what she had just said. Her brain really *was* on the fritz. She had almost forgotten the previous plan to meet the girls at Game of Flats after dinner. She had been enjoying her time with Lauren so much that it had completely slipped her mind.

"What's wrong?" Lauren stopped walking and ran her concerned gaze over Penny, as if inspecting her from head to toe to determine what had caused the reaction.

"No, nothing. It's just…" Penny bit her lip and considered her options. She had practically begged Mara and the others to join her at the Flats to drown her sorrows, and like the good friends they were, they had dropped any plans they had to make it happen. She couldn't blow them off because she was intrigued by some woman she had just met.

On the other hand, Lauren had proven to be more than just some woman her mother used to know. She was someone who really held Penny's interest, someone Penny wanted to know better, not just for the family history she was providing, but because she genuinely *liked* her. She met Lauren's gaze again and heat curled down her spine. She liked a lot of things about her. Maybe there was a compromise. She tipped her head and regarded Lauren thoughtfully. "Do you have any other plans tonight?"

Lauren's finely sculpted left eyebrow arched up as if her curiosity was piqued by the question. "Nothing at all. What did you have in mind?"

Penny felt her expression relax. She could have the best of both worlds after all. "How do you feel about lesbian bars?"

"Favorable." Lauren winked. "I've met a lot of ladies that way."

A shiver tickled its way up the back of Penny's neck. It wasn't the response she expected, but it sure seemed…favorable.

CHAPTER FOUR

Game of Flats was exactly what Lauren had pictured it to be—dim lighting, loud music and tons of young women crammed on the dance floor showing off for one another. The lesbian bar scene had not changed much since her own clubbing days.

Lauren sat with Penny and her friend Jenna at the bar on vinyl stools that had seen better days. Lauren had been fortunate enough to grab one that wasn't sticky, but she had wiped it down with a sanitizing wipe she produced from her purse, much to the snickers and eyerolls of the other patrons around them. They were still waiting for the rest of their group to arrive at the bar, but the three had gotten a head start on the alcohol consumption.

A second round of tequila shots was already lined up in front of the trio, and although Lauren had kept up with the younger women tossing them back, she was a beer behind them. *Oh, to be in your thirties*. Those girls had no idea how time would march across their bodies and affect their tolerance for alcohol, among other things.

Jenna, Penny's friend with the bold, brassy personality that matched her dark, short-cropped faux-hawk hairstyle, was doing her best to keep up the spirits of their little group. Between Penny's work news and Lauren's post-breakup funk, it had been no small task. "Okay, okay. This time a toast—to Lauren's vacation."

"To vacation," they echoed, but with much less enthusiasm.

The burning liquid slid down Lauren's throat, and she squinted her watering eyes at the bitter aftertaste. A shiver worked its way from her shoulders down her spine and she let out a *yelp*.

Penny laughed, but she was waving her stiffly held hands in front of her face like her own throat was on fire, so she wasn't completely unaffected by the alcohol. Penny truly was a beautiful woman, even with her long, blond hair mussed from the dozen or so times she had dug her fingertips into it and tugged in frustration.

"I still can't believe I'm sitting here doing shots with Lauren Hansen." Jenna slapped a palm to her forehead.

"I still can't believe you recognized my name," Lauren countered.

"Are you kidding me?" Jenna's eyes went wide. "My gallery would love to have pieces from a photographer of your caliber. I can't wait until the next time I work there so I can brag about meeting you."

"Oh my god." Penny pulled on her locks again, only stopping to chase the tequila with a big swig of beer. "What the hell am I going to do without work? Work is all I do."

"Honey." Lauren put her hand on the middle of Penny's back and gave her a reassuring rub. "Work isn't all you do. You just go ahead and take some time away. Don't even go near that casino. Stay at home if you want, but find something else to do. Maybe take up a new hobby."

Penny's head dropped dramatically to the bar in front of her.

Jenna leaned in close to Lauren and spoke right into her ear. "Um, you know Penny lives in the casino, right? It's literally all she does."

"Well, crap." Lauren rubbed faster like that would fix the situation. Of course she knew that. She had enjoyed sidecars earlier in Penny's undecorated suite. Maybe she could use the time to fix her décor. "You need a break from that place. Do you have any family you can go visit?"

Penny shook her head glumly.

"Lauren, the casino is her family business," Jenna whispered yet again. "Her whole family lives here."

"It's okay, it's okay, it's okay." Penny picked her head back up, clearly not okay. She took another long pull on her beer bottle before continuing in a slightly slurred voice. "Look at me, going on and on about my pity party, when you, Lauren, are starting your vacation. Something wonderful and exciting. Enough about my crap. Tell us about your trip."

"Oh, the trip." Lauren sighed and took a big sip of her own beer. The alcohol was doing nothing to improve her mood, but she kept downing it anyway. Sharing her story might take some of the spotlight off Penny's woes. She ran a finger through the condensation on her beer bottle and pressed on. "I probably should have canceled my plans. I almost turned around in the airport and just went home. Going on what was supposed to be an anniversary trip alone was a stupid idea."

The closer Lauren got to departing for the resort, the more she really believed that. It wasn't too late. She could still decide not to get on that plane. She could hang out in Vegas for a few days, or she could just go home and get back to moping around the house wondering how this all happened. She *did* need to get her butt in gear with her photography. She was all set for the upcoming show, but her creativity had taken a complete nosedive since the breakup with Carolyn. She hadn't felt like working on anything new in several months. Inspiration had left the building.

"But you already paid for the trip," Jenna argued, but her face was full of pity, as if she felt sorry for Lauren giving up on her vacation. "Besides, it's just like you were saying to Penny. It will do you good to have a change of scenery. Who knows? Maybe you'll actually have a good time."

"There would be a better chance of me having a good time if I wasn't going alone."

"Well, don't look at me," Jenna smirked. "I can't just blow town on a whim. I've got to work."

"I don't have to work." Penny raised a hand as if beckoning a teacher to call on her, and gave a staccato, bitter laugh. The alcohol was really having its way with her. "There's the bright side to this mess. I can *totally* blow town on a whim."

"Oh my god!" Jenna's voice was an amused hoot. "You should totally go with Lauren on the trip!"

"No, I didn't mean…" Penny's eyes went wide. A blush crept up her cheeks and across that beautiful face, clearly embarrassed at the implication.

"You should go with her, Penny. Really," Jenna continued despite the look of utter disbelief Lauren was attempting to convey.

Lauren shook her head and waved a palm in front of her as she took a hard swallow of beer. Jenna, a twenty-something Lauren had met less than two hours ago, wanted her to go on a vacation for a week with a woman she barely knew. *Young people.*

"I mean, why not?" Jenna pushed. "You don't want to go alone. Penny needs to get out of town. It's the perfect arrangement."

Lauren opened her mouth to argue, but suddenly paused. She *had* said repeatedly she didn't want to go on that trip alone, and she could do a lot worse for a travel buddy than smart, sophisticated Penny Rothmoor. They could spend the week poolside, lay low and heal their hurting hearts. Or, really, they didn't need to spend any time together at all. It was a big resort. They could each go their own way and just share the suite. Even the accommodations were big enough that they wouldn't be tripping over each other. Lauren had booked the honeymoon suite for the trip with Carolyn, going full-out for a person who totally betrayed her. She had been an idiot.

"I could never impose like that," Penny insisted, although the bitterness had melted from her expression and she looked calmer than she had all night. Maybe this was exactly what Penny needed too—a damn getaway from their normal lives.

"It *is* a vacation for two, and it *is* paid for," Lauren pointed out with a shrug. With the tension gone from Penny's features, she was absolutely glowing. Longing whispered through Lauren as she looked at her in this new light. Having a travel companion was sounding better and better. "You would only need to get a flight."

"I would like to get away from the Rothmoor for a bit." Penny sucked down the last of her beer and signaled to the bartender for another. "You wouldn't mind, really?"

The relief on Penny's face at the mention of getting away warmed Lauren. Or maybe the warmth was due to the way she had chugged her drink while agreeing to this Lucy-and-Ethel-style plan. Surely the alcohol was responsible for the surge of attraction that zapped through her body at the thought of spending a week in close quarters with Penny. "I wouldn't mind at all."

Jenna, the travel matchmaker, let out a whoop and then promptly ordered another round of shots. "You two are gonna have so much fun, and you'll come back refreshed and ready to take on the world again."

Lauren wasn't sure she would ever be ready to take on the world again, but a little fun would probably do her some good. This time when Jenna raised her glass and repeated her cheerful toast, Lauren's response was much more heartfelt. "To vacation!"

CHAPTER FIVE

Penny woke up the next morning and slowly rolled over in her king-size bed. The room was still dark thanks to blackout curtains. At least she had had the good sense to shut them before she passed out for the night. She was still wearing the jeans and bra she had worn to the bar the night before and her head was pounding. *What the hell time of day was it?* Her hair stunk of cigarette smoke—a hazard of hanging out at Game of Flats, and a few strands of it were stuck to her cheek, glued in place by either sweat or drool. It was hard to determine which.

I have to get to work!

She sat up in bed quickly and immediately regretted it. A dull, persistent thud made its presence known smack in the middle of her forehead. *Damn tequila.* Her stomach roiled at the memory of that fourth shot—and at the reason she had been at the bar in the first place. She did *not* have to get to work. She had no work. She was suspended from her position until her father decided otherwise. Her heart twisted in her chest.

Dropping to the mattress, she rolled over and buried her head under the pillows. The coolness of the sheets was sweet relief against her sweaty skin, giving her a brief moment of clarity to think. She didn't have to go to work, but she did need to get up and face the world. There was something she was supposed to do. Something she told the others she would do when they were at the bar last night before Mara and Frankie had showed up.

She spun around and popped up to a sitting position like a giant, hungover Jack-in-the-box. She had agreed to go on vacation with Lauren Hansen to the Waverly Winds Resort! Her head throbbed again in response to the sudden movement. Why had she agreed to that? She would have to pack, and book a flight, and…leave her bed. It was a crazy idea on the most basic level. Not to mention she didn't even know Lauren.

Until a few days ago Lauren was just a character in a bunch of teenage adventure tall tales. The stuff of legends. Practically a figment of her imagination. The alcohol had messed with her clarity of thought, giving her a false attraction to Lauren as well as a fractured logic that had led to her agreeing to the trip.

Not that she wasn't glad she'd met Lauren, but she hadn't expected her to be so…gorgeous. Lauren had a certain polish to her. A radiance. She had long, beautiful hair that danced across her shoulders when she threw back a shot. Plus she was a good enough sport to join the girls in throwing back shots. And her nails, although clipped short, were professionally manicured and done in a cheery shade of hot pink. Penny had always been partial to femmes. Of course, none of this added up to her knowing Lauren well enough to go on a week's vacation with her. What the hell had she been thinking?

Oh yeah, tequila.

She could bow out gracefully. She could just call Lauren and explain. She couldn't run away from her problems anyway, even if she tried. Going to Hawaii wouldn't solve anything. She reached for her phone on the nightstand, finally noticing the time on the digital clock—ten forty-five. She never slept that late. Girls' night out had really done a number on her. Maybe it was just the stress of everything. Losing her fiancé and her job, which was basically her entire identity, all at once. Depression might very well be setting in. *So damn pathetic.*

At the last moment she hit the button to dial up Jenna instead of Lauren. Jenna would agree. There had to be some kind of hall pass for a decision made after a large quantity of tequila. Jenna always knew what to do in any situation. She would know the best way for Penny to break the news to Lauren.

Jenna picked up on the third ring. "Hey, what's going on? Please tell me you didn't just wake up. You hung over?" She always went full speed, loud and lively, with a laugh that made you want to join in, even when your head was going to explode from excessive alcohol consumption.

"Yeah, I'm pretty hung. I feel like I've wasted half the day."

"Screw that!" Jenna boomed. "You're on vacation. Did you get a flight?"

"About that..." Penny rubbed her temples, willing her headache to take a hike. "I don't think I'm gonna go, Jenna."

"What? You have to go. You already told Lauren you would. Her flight left first thing this morning. She's probably already there." Jenna's voice was so thick with disappointment you would have thought Penny was sending *her* to the Waverly Winds Resort alone.

"I can't leave the Rothmoor. Not now," Penny protested. "Maybe my father realized suspending me was a mistake. What if he changes his mind and I'm not here? Potential disaster."

"Penny, if he changes his mind, you'll fly back. No big deal." Jenna's tone turned flat, bored with Penny's arguments, which she obviously found completely invalid. "Besides, when was the last time your father changed his mind once he made a decision? Get your ass packed and get a flight. It's a free vacation for fuck's sake."

"So what? I don't even care about that." It was a crappy thing to say to Jenna, and Penny winced in shame the second the words were out of her mouth. Not everybody had the financial benefit of coming from a family who owned a casino in Las Vegas. Jenna worked two jobs to make ends meet. She would probably jump face first at an opportunity like this. No, Jenna did not have financial support from her family, but she did have the emotional support of a mother who loved her no matter what, a parent who would have never sent their henchman to gleefully put her on leave from work indefinitely.

Penny's temples throbbed again at the indignity of her job situation. Just because she was feeling crappy about work didn't mean she had to act that way to her friends. Her shoulders slumped in shame as she made a feeble attempt to recover from her careless remark. "It's just that I don't even know this woman."

"A week on the beach with a hot chick like Lauren doesn't sound too shabby to me. Go with her. Book your damn flight. It beats the hell out of sitting around your suite feeling sorry for yourself."

"I am not feeling sorry for myself."

"Whatever, dude. Have a good trip." She clicked off the call before Penny could get in another word.

She frowned as she gingerly sat up and swung her legs over the edge of the bed. Jenna was supposed to back her up on bailing out of this half-baked vacation plan, not encourage her to go along with it. It didn't matter. She wasn't going to go on a trip with a woman she hardly knew —hot or not—and that was that.

Jenna was wrong anyway. Penny wasn't feeling sorry for herself. Or at least she wouldn't be once she stopped the hammering inside her skull. She plucked at her sweat-soaked tank top. Damn alcohol sweats. She needed sustenance, coffee, and a greasy breakfast sandwich. That would be a good start. Bacon would make everything better.

Five minutes later, with a thin pink hoodie zipped up over her tank and a ball cap pulled low on her head, she ventured out of the elevator and into the casino in search of food. She kept her eyes down as she scooted through the lobby to the coffee shop just inside the game play area.

"Your usual, Ms. Rothmoor?" Kris, the chipper woman who had worked the weekend morning shift at the shop for the past six years, smiled brightly as Penny approached the counter. Her disguise wasn't quite as airtight as she had hoped.

Her usual, a yogurt cup with fresh berries, was not going to cut it. Only the greasy goodness of a breakfast sandwich would ease her hangover. "I'm shaking it up today, Kris. Bacon, egg, and cheese bagel with a large coffee, please."

Kris raised her eyebrows in surprise but then nodded. She poured her a tall cup of coffee and set off to prepare the rest of her order.

Penny tapped her foot as she waited and silently thanked her lucky stars that she had managed to avoid any other familiar faces on her journey. The dull thumping in her head wasn't conducive to making friendly conversation. The sooner she could get back into her bed and curl up in her sheets, the better. She would eat her breakfast, take a little nap, and all would be right with the world again. Not the job part, but the pounding headache part at least. One step at a time. She paid for her food and took a careful sip of her steamy beverage. That was when she saw him out of the corner of her eye.

Her father.

Dressed in a gray suit with a silver sheen, looking sharp as ever, his stride proud and confident, he was heading right her way. She quickly turned back toward the counter, but in her haste to avoid being seen, she jostled her cup. The coffee sloshed over the rim and splashed down the front of her sweatshirt.

"Damn it." She tugged her cap down further and dabbed a paper napkin at her chest. The last thing she needed while hungover was to run into her dad and talk about the job she had been asked to keep away from. She would apologize to him properly once she was able to shake the shame that had settled over her since she lost her cool on the casino floor and regained some semblance of her professionalism. For now she would lie low.

She tossed the balled up napkin into the trash before grabbing her sandwich in one hand and her coffee in the other, and making a beeline for the elevator across the lobby. She had almost made it past the front desk when her path was cut off by another man in a smart suit calling out orders to a bellhop.

Timothy.

Could the morning get any worse?

With a swift pivot that rivaled the smooth court moves of a WNBA player, she spun to her left and ducked into the back hallway to take the stairs up a floor where she could wait on the elevator in peace, away from the bustling crowd in the lobby.

Needing to get away from the tourists, away from Timothy, and away from her father, she slipped into an elevator car and punched the button for the fourteenth floor. Her heart was still racing from her near misses as she leaned back against the wall and sucked in a deep breath. She was getting pretty good at ducking out of sight at just the right moment, but keeping it up every time she left her suite for the next couple of weeks during the mandatory vacation time was going to be exhausting.

She could picture how smug Timothy would be and how dismayed her father would be if either of them spotted her in the casino just then. She was wearing the clothes she had worn out to a bar the night before. Her bed head was tucked hastily into a baseball cap, and there was coffee spilled down the front of her hoodie. Her face went hot with embarrassment. She couldn't keep this up.

There was one quick and easy solution to all of it. She could avoid the both of them if she was in Hawaii for the next week. Free trip...hot chick. A wave of resolution washed over her. Suddenly the only thing she desperately needed was to get back to her suite and start packing.

She was going on vacation.

CHAPTER SIX

The Waverly Winds Resort was a welcome sight after six hungover hours on a plane and almost thirty still mildly nauseous minutes in a cab. Penny should have gone with the hair of the dog back in the airport in Vegas. Instead, she had been chugging Sport-Ade and hoping to keep the complimentary in-flight nuts down.

She hoisted her carry-on and dragged her rolling case behind her. She had packed light for the week, figuring most of her time would be spent poolside. If she didn't feel like dressing and going to dinner, screw it, she wouldn't. She could always order room service and not even have to leave the room.

The large white stucco, red-slate roofed building was imposing and inviting all at once. It summed up her feelings about the trip. She wanted to relax, but she worried she would be caught under the shadow of what might be happening at the Rothmoor while she was gone. Gaping up at the exterior architecture of the resort was doing nothing for the tension still lingering in her upper back. Rolling her neck and pressing her lips together resolutely, she approached the entrance to the building.

Inside the etched glass sliding doors she was greeted by a blast of icy cold air that felt like heaven to her hangover sweats. She was also greeted by a pair of hunky, tanned, shirtless doormen with intensely white smiles. Paddled ceiling fans circled lazily overhead as she rolled her luggage over the terra-cotta tile floor.

Across the lobby, Lauren sat on white wicker furniture with palm-leaf printed cushions. The bright orange, turquoise, and hot pink print of her long, flowing caftan dress was striking on her. Her brown hair was swept up into a messy bun held in place with hairsticks, exposing her long, sexy neck. Penny waved as she approached and swallowed hard against the stirring in her core. Lauren stretched her arms open as she stood to greet her.

"You made it! I was worried you would change your mind." Lauren rubbed a hand across Penny's upper back, making Penny feel instantly at home in her arms. Penny could understand why her mother always held her friend so dear. Lauren had a real gift for making people comfortable. "I've already checked in, so we can take your bags straight up to the room."

Lauren took the rolling case from her before leading her down the corridor to the bank of elevators. The honeymoon suite was on the eighteenth floor, and Lauren chattered away the entire ride, describing in great detail the various amenities she had discovered at the resort since her arrival. Once inside their room, Lauren flung her arms wide again. "Make yourself at home."

Penny dropped her bag by the sofa and took in her surroundings. The main room had everything one would expect. It was spacious, but nothing out of the ordinary. She ran her fingertips against the deep green and tan leafy print fabric of the sofa. Typical, *you're on vacation—relax* stuff. Much more calming than the sleek décor of the rooms at the Rothmoor. "This is really nice. Thank you so much for inviting me."

"Thank you for coming along. Oh, check this out." Lauren led her through the French doors separating the common space from the bedroom.

Penny skirted the king-size bed and large bamboo dresser to get a peek at a Jacuzzi. She imagined the tub was what set the honeymoon suite apart from the everyday room at the Waverly Winds. She also imagined—ever so briefly—her and Lauren relaxing together in the tub. She quickly crossed her arms in front of her chest to hide her budding nipples. "Well that's... something."

Hoping to shake her lustful thoughts, she moved toward the gauzy curtain-covered sliding door that led onto the balcony overlooking the sparkling Hawaiian coast. She poked her head out long enough to get a good whiff of sea breeze, a scent she had always found calming. Her spirits picked up at the thought of lounging in the sunshine and dipping her toes in the surf.

"It's a nice view, isn't it?" Lauren stood behind her peering over her shoulder. "So serene."

"It's stunning," Penny agreed, facing her new friend. But when she did, heat prickled in her cheeks. She was standing with a woman she barely knew in a bedroom with a giant bed and hot tub that screamed SEX. *Awkward.* "I'll take the couch?" she blurted, as if she needed to clarify the sleeping arrangements.

"It pulls out." Lauren rolled with the change of subject. "Do you want to grab a drink?"

Penny smiled, relieved to be back on familiar ground with Lauren. "As long as it's not tequila."

"Put on your suit. Poolside special is rum runners today."

Fifteen minutes later the women were reclining side-by-side, tall glasses of rum-infused fruit punch garnished with tiny umbrellas in hand.

"This is the life," Penny sighed between sips through the neon green twisty straw poking out of her drink. For the first time since she had opened her eyes that morning, she was finally able to relax.

"It sure is." Lauren adjusted her floppy wide-brimmed hat, then stretched her arms down at her sides, basking in the sun.

Penny glanced down at her pale-white legs and frowned. "I have really neglected my tan lately. I've kinda been on an 'all work, no play' streak."

"While trying to fix the situation that blew up anyway?" Lauren's eyes were hidden under that brim, but her tone remained even despite the irony of her statement.

Penny considered Lauren's words. She had always been super committed to her career since her dream had been to take over the family business one day. When she was a kid, her father would give her tasks to complete for him. Then she moved up to working at the restaurants as a teenager. When she was in college, she spent summers interning so she would be ready to accept her role as Floor Manager after graduation. But that wasn't the real reason she had buried herself in work the past several months, and looking back on it now, the truth was evident.

"No," she admitted with another sigh strong enough to make the tiny festive umbrella in her drink circle the rim of the glass. "I was avoiding my relationship with Bryce. And then that blew up, causing the blowup at work. My dad is right. This whole mess is really all my fault."

"How can it all be your fault?" Lauren lifted her floppy brim with her slender fingers to peer at Penny. "It's a big company, a big business. I'm sure your role is very important there, but you're only one person. You can't control other people's choices or actions. And your father can't possibly expect that of you."

"Things went south with Bryce, and instead of dealing with it, I put my head down and became a workaholic. And look what that got me? Now I've got no work and no relationship with a fiancé to face, just a hell of a lot of nothing. What if I go back to Vegas and find out I've lost my job for good? What the fuck will I do with myself?" The sting of tears made her grateful for her oversize sunglasses. She was sitting poolside on a gifted vacation and she was crying.

"Hey." Lauren snapped her fingers to get Penny's attention. "That's not going to happen. Your father will sort out what he needs to sort out, and when you get back you will return to your position at the casino and fight like hell to do your best work. Just like you always have."

"But—"

"No buts." Lauren's tone was stern, no-nonsense. "If you go back to Vegas and the world doesn't look like you expect, you will figure it out then. You're a young woman with your whole life ahead of you. Believe me, *you'll figure it out.* But you're not going to spend your week of vacation worrying about it. No way. We had a pact: to get away from that crap, and by golly, I'm making you stick to it."

"We had a pact?" Penny bit her bottom lip to keep from laughing about the *by golly* in the middle of Lauren's tough love speech.

"We did." Lauren nodded firmly as she shifted on her lounger. "We had a pact. We toasted on it, remember? To vacation!"

"That qualifies as a pact?" Penny's tears were forgotten as she peered over the edge of her sunglasses at her new friend. "Two words over a tequila shot?"

"That's right, and we're both sticking to it."

"Both? I guess that's fair." She shrugged. She could *try* not to think about the Rothmoor. She *could* just live in the moment and enjoy her time off. Possibly.

"That means no work calls." Lauren pointed an accusing finger at Penny as if sensing her doubt. "I'm serious. No calls, texts, emails, whatever. No work at all. And *absolutely* no contact with Bryce."

"Ha." Penny's laugh was a bitter honk that came out much louder than she intended. She covered her mouth with her hand. Maybe she should slow down on the rum runner. "No problem with that. My dad took my old phone and provided me with a brand-new one. New number and all. 'For security reasons,' he said."

"Good." Lauren nodded again. "No drama."

"But what about you?" Penny demanded. "What about your end of the pact?"

"Look at me." Lauren spread her arms open over her tanned and toned body. "I'm relaxing."

"Sure you are. On the outside." Sunlight played on Lauren's shoulders highlighting the smattering of freckles there that

Penny hadn't noticed before. A tickle worked its way down Penny's spine. She fidgeted in her chair and crossed her legs. "But you need some stakes in this too. Maybe you need a new phone."

"I'm not taking time out of my vacation to do that." She shook her head adamantly. "Besides. No need. I have no desire to reach out to anyone."

"What if Carolyn reaches out to you?" Penny challenged. "You can't give in to drama either."

"No drama. Carolyn won't reach out," Lauren said simply. "She moved on. That's what the whole issue was. That's why we split."

"But she could. You need to hold up your end of the bargain. Delete her number."

"Oh, Penny. I can't delete her number, as much as I would love to." Lauren gave her a sad smile. "We lived together for a long time. We're still dividing up the crap."

"For the week. Block her. Block her number."

"I can do that?" Lauren grabbed her phone from the glass table between them. "I can just block her for the week?"

"Hell, yes." Penny sat up and faced Lauren. "Here. Let me show you." She took the smartphone and punched a few buttons. "Done, and…done."

"Just like that?" Lauren took the phone back and stared at it quizzically.

"Just like that." Penny returned to her original position on the lounger. To her surprise a sense of calm washed over her once again. If Lauren could do it, she could do it too. She just needed to set her mind to it. A week of mindless vacation was a good thing. Lauren was right. She would return to the Rothmoor refreshed and ready to get right back into it.

Suddenly a cool shadow cast itself across her happy thoughts. Literally. Penny opened her eyes to see the shade was the result of a hunky, dark-haired guy holding a tray with two full champagne flutes.

"Champagne for the happy couple?" The hunk spoke in a vaguely foreign accent that sounded fake.

"Um, what?" Lauren lifted her brim again.

"Champagne." He repeated in his totally fake and cheesy Waverly Winds accent. "It's your anniversary, no?"

Sadness flickered briefly over Lauren's face before her expression shifted to mischievous, and she arched a *why the hell not?* eyebrow in Penny's direction. "Yes, thank you." Her tone was bright as she accepted a champagne flute from the tray and nodded at Penny to do the same.

Of course, that meant Penny had a drink in each hand. "To vacation!" she toasted before taking a sip of bubbly.

"To vacation." Lauren grinned. The pact was in full swing.

"Enjoy." The hunk bowed slightly. "My name is Paolo. If I can be of any service during your stay, do not hesitate to ask."

"Thank you, Paolo," Lauren sing-songed as he walked away. When he was out of earshot, she turned back to Penny. "Hey, I paid for the anniversary package. We may as well get my money's worth."

"I'm all for perks," Penny agreed gleefully. She could "happy couple" it with the best of them. "Bring it on, Waverly Winds."

Just like that, Penny was celebrating an anniversary with a woman she had known for all of twenty-four hours.

CHAPTER SEVEN

For the first two days of their stay at the Waverly Winds, Penny had gone along with Lauren in her effort to take advantage of every anniversary trip benefit that had come their way. Lauren took this as a good indicator of Penny's sense of adventure. After the complimentary champagne at the pool on Sunday afternoon, they had returned to the room to find a huge bouquet of fresh flowers on the sideboard with a note of congratulations from the Waverly Winds Resort staff. They clipped their favorites from the bunch and wore them in their hair when they went to dinner that evening, where they were treated to the richest and gooiest chocolate desserts Lauren had ever experienced—on the house.

But Lauren dragging Penny to the Waverly Winds moonlight pool party might have been one adventure too many. The women sat on the opposite side of the water from where they had lounged earlier in the day, flowers still in their hair. Lauren surveyed their surroundings, from tiki torches and open-shirted staff members in leis, to a deejay playing Beach

Boys songs, the ambience was completely on-brand for the resort—over the top and kitschy as heck.

"Don't get me wrong, I appreciate that you brought me along. It does beat the hell out of moping around at home." Penny shook her head. "But this resort is the cheesiest place I've ever been. And I live in Vegas, so that's saying something."

The light of the moon rippled across the surface of the pool, and illuminated Penny as she leaned back in the lounger. Her blond hair shimmered like a halo around her head. She was dressed in a long gray, white, and black dress that was form-fitting and showed a peek of her cleavage. Not that Lauren was looking. Even as Penny rolled her eyes and her voice dripped with sarcasm, she remained the picture of beauty. Lauren raised her camera to take a few shots of Penny glowing in the moonlight.

"Agreed. Although they keep giving us free stuff, and that's not so bad." Lauren lowered her lens to address Penny without the filter between them. "And look at those couples on the dance floor. Look at the pure joy on their faces as they let their regular lives go and become vacation people."

Penny shrugged. "Yolo."

"What?"

"You only live once," Penny explained with a grin.

"Exactly." Lauren regarded Penny in her long dress and strappy sandals. If they were going to keep the vacation pact, they had to let go and be vacation people. "We should be like these people. We *need* to be like these people. Shall we dance?"

Penny kicked her feet in the air to propel herself out of the lounger. Lauren snapped a few more shots of her as she stretched her arms above her head. "We shall. Put that camera down and let's boogie."

Lauren did as she was told, asked Paolo to keep her camera behind the bar, and followed Penny onto the dance floor, a makeshift wooden surface reserved for grooving and moving at the far end of the pool. Navigating through the other revelers, they found a space just big enough for the two of them to let loose. She shook her shoulders along to the Jan and Dean song blaring from the speakers surrounding them. Penny had also begun to sway to the music. The muscles in her arms flexed, displaying their full definition, and a distinct heat pooled between Lauren's legs. There was no doubt in her mind that her dance partner was the most gorgeous woman on the floor.

Penny presented herself as a picture of poise, and when she moved she had a natural grace, her long limbs swaying in time to the beat of the music. She attracted quite a bit of attention from the dancers around them, women and men alike casting admiring glances her way. Lauren was going to have to step up her game if she was going to keep up with Vacation Penny.

As the music changed again, the deejay's voice boomed over the sound system. "Ladies and gentlemen on the dance floor, clear the way for our party crew, and get ready to limbo! How low can you go?"

"I'm shaking my ass in public to sixties surfer music surrounded by silver-haired dudes in flowered shirts unbuttoned much too far. That's pretty low for me." Penny leaned in and giggled in Lauren's ear. "But damn it, I bet I can go lower."

Poise and wit. Lauren liked this girl. The heat of Penny's breath lingered on Lauren's ear, causing a shiver to work its way down her spine.

"So you're going to compete?"

"You and me both. We're vacation people."

Lauren couldn't say no to that smile, not to mention she was the one who started the vacation people thing in the first place. Her back would probably hate her in the morning, but hell, maybe they could get free anniversary trip massages at the resort spa. "Okay, I'm in. Lead the way."

For the first two rounds Lauren shimmied under the bar with the best of them, but by the third time around the limbo did her in. She wasn't alone. A bunch of the competition dropped like flies. Penny, however, slid right under the bar, moving on to the next round.

Out of the game, Lauren grabbed her camera and began snapping away again. The crowd was cheering on the remaining contestants while the Limbo song played over and over again.

Penny hung on until it was down to her and one young guy who was part of a bachelor party. The guy was handsome with a head of messy, thick hair, several leis stacked around his neck, and sunglasses covering his eyes, even though it was dark enough that he could most likely not see a damn thing through them.

The game went on two more rounds before Mr. Sunglasses gave in to the pressure and dropped to the ground on his attempt to shimmy under the bar. The onlookers cheered as Penny raised her arms in the air celebrating her victory. Even her opponent applauded before picking her up and twirling her around in an overdone show of masculine congratulations. When he placed her back on her feet, he removed his shades and leaned in close to speak in her ear. Penny pulled away and he typed something into his phone. It was easy for Lauren to surmise she had given him her number.

Penny's face was glowing with joy as she returned to Lauren's side. "How about that for a vacation person?"

"Well done. You were a star." Lauren slung an arm around Penny's shoulders and pulled her into a quick mini hug, but the image of Mr. Sunglasses getting those digits was still niggling at her brain. "And you made a friend too."

Penny scrunched up her eyebrows for a moment before realization crossed her features. "Scott? Oh yeah. He's here with his friends for a bachelor party vacation. His big brother is getting married. I gave him my number to be polite, but I'm not interested. Fun guy, though."

"You're not interested?" Lauren raised a curious eyebrow. "You don't even know him."

Penny shook her head. "No. He reminds me too much of Bryce, my ex. Big, burly football player type. I'm just…turned off by it right now."

"I can understand that." She put a sympathetic hand on Penny's muscular upper arm. No wonder Penny had rocked the limbo. Her whole body was toned and taut. "I wouldn't want to get involved with anyone who reminded me of Carolyn."

The beach party music started up again, and the women stood on the fringe of the crowd watching as dancers returned to lose themselves in the fun. Suddenly Lauren wasn't feeling it anymore, and it must have plainly showed on her face.

"Hey." Penny bumped her shoulder into Lauren's. "I didn't mean to bring up our exes. I've broken the vacation pact, haven't I?"

"Absolutely not!" If Penny had broken the pact so had Lauren, and she refused to break the spell so early in the week. Surely they could make it more than two days. She fixed her lips into a weary smile. "I'm just worn out. I think I'm going to head back to the room."

"Same here. Let's call it a night. We've got a whole relaxing week in front of us. No need to run ourselves into the ground on day two."

Lauren linked her arm with Penny's and steered her back to the hotel. Penny was right. They had a lot of time ahead of them. And when Penny tipped her head onto Lauren's shoulder as they walked along, Lauren was very glad they did.

CHAPTER EIGHT

Penny woke up the next morning with the worst crick in her back compliments of the damn pullout sofa bed. Or maybe it was too much limbo. Most likely a combination of the two. In spite of the pain, she grinned at the memory of the previous night—the crowd and Lauren cheering her on. Somehow it was the second part that warmed her and gave her a fluttering in her belly. She *liked* impressing Lauren.

She was really looking forward to the day they had planned, just relaxing on the beach together. Penny had picked out a new bikini for the day, and she had the latest issues of her favorite magazines already packed in her beach bag, totally ready for some lounging in the sun. But when she rolled over to get out of bed, the ache burned up between her shoulder blades. She let out a yelp loud enough that it was heard in the other room.

"Is everything okay out there?" Lauren called in a sleepy voice, as if she had just awakened from a deep slumber.

"I'm fine," Penny replied as she bent forward to stretch. Her cheeks flushed with embarrassment. So much for her smooth limbo champion image. There was nothing sexy about not being able to bear the aches and pains of being over thirty with grace. "I just slept funny and twisted my back."

Penny let her arms dangle and took several breaths in and out before slowly rolling up to a straight position. As she did, she spotted Lauren leaning against the frame of the door to the bedroom wearing a cute shorts and button-up top pajama set. She was watching her, studying her carefully.

"Any better?" Lauren smiled sympathetically. Even with bedhead she somehow looked put together, composed.

"Not much." Penny grimaced. "But I'll survive."

"Okay. First things first. Sit back down on the bed," Lauren commanded as she joined Penny on the pullout. Her take-charge tone caused a fizzle of excitement to erupt in Penny's middle. "Well, crap, no wonder you're sore. This bed is the pits."

"I don't know." Penny managed after a gasp and groan as Lauren's hands made contact with her upper back. Lauren's fingers dug into her flesh, rubbing at the sore muscles. "I was thinking maybe I was just too old to limbo anymore."

Lauren let out a low laugh. "You? Hell no. Don't you be giving up on dance contests any time soon. You have many years of the limbo ahead of you."

"Mmm." Penny rolled her head forward. She exhaled slowly as her back began to relax in the care of Lauren's magic touch. "I hope you're right."

"I know I'm right." Lauren's voice was a low, calming purr. "A body like this isn't going to give out on you any time soon. You've got a gorgeous back, by the way. Beautiful posture."

Was Lauren *flirting* with her?

"Many years of ballet lessons as a kid paid off. Thank you." Penny sighed happily. "You've got amazing hands."

Was she flirting back? With her *mom's friend?* No. Lauren was most likely just trying to keep the mood light in the name of the vacation pact. Keeping spirits up and all that.

"Glad to help." Lauren gently ran her hands down Penny's spine one last time before standing. Penny longed for her touch again the second it was lost. "Now for step two. I'm making us appointments for a proper massage at the spa."

As Lauren ducked back into her room to make the call, Penny got to work putting the couch back together. She wouldn't mind a spa day, but she felt better already after having Lauren's capable hands working her muscles.

When Penny finished with the couch, she started some coffee in the little machine on the desk. It wouldn't be gourmet, but she needed a shot of caffeine.

"So the spa was booked solid for today, but I got us an appointment for tomorrow morning. It's a couples' massage, so I hope you don't mind. I figured we could keep on rolling with the anniversary trip thing. Maybe they'll throw in a few complimentary perks. Who knows?"

"I don't mind at all." Penny grinned and passed her a mug of subpar coffee. She could think of worse ways to spend a morning than relaxing half naked with a beautiful woman. A couples' massage with Lauren was more than fine by her. "I'm totally down to roll with it."

CHAPTER NINE

Penny sat in the late morning sun, her heels planted in the warm sand just past the end of her beach towel. Earlier she had stood on the edge of the water next to Lauren, the rush of the fizzling waves splashing over their feet and ankles. They had spotted dolphins farther out, and watched in awe as they jumped in arcs breaking up the horizon. There were moments when the majesty of nature took one's breath away. The sight of dolphins frolicking across the sparkling surface of the Pacific Ocean was certainly one of them. Penny had relished the feeling, and let calm descend upon her. That was what vacation was all about. Maybe she was finally catching on to the vacation people thing after all.

Lauren had remained on the edge of the surf snapping pictures after that, but Penny had returned to her beach towel and settled in. Perusing the latest glossy issue of her favorite fashion mag seemed like the perfect way to pass the morning.

Now Penny dug her heels further into the sand. She rubbed them back and forth against the grains and did her best to ignore any thoughts of dirt, crab parts, and sea debris the beach surface contained. Instead she reminded herself of the exfoliating benefits of sand on skin. It was practically a natural spa treatment.

That was the kind of spin and marketing she used in her job at the casino. Her father called it "readjusting perspective," except she wasn't supposed to be thinking about work. Not even tiny thoughts like that one. She had made a promise to Lauren and she was going to do her damnedest to keep it.

She shielded her eyes from the sun with her flattened palm and looked out to the edge of the surf where Lauren was still snapping shots with her trusty camera. The outline of her trim, toned figure against the glistening sea held Penny's attention. She noticed the firm definition of Lauren's arms as she pointed her lens in one direction then the next.

The memory of Lauren's strong hands and long fingers moving deftly over her back that morning set off another flutter of excitement in her belly. It quickly traveled down between her legs, resulting in a pussy clench that caught her completely off guard.

It was Lauren giving her the sex shivers. *Her mother's friend.* Although, in all fairness, Penny didn't really know Lauren at all until she met her in person two days ago. Before that, she had only known the name Lauren Hansen as some kind of legend from days of yore. Her mother had told her stories about their teenage adventures. That had been the extent of Penny's familiarity with Lauren—the sidekick in her mother's buddy-trip tales. Now Lauren was starring in Penny's mid-morning backrub fantasies.

As if Lauren could sense she was the focus of Penny's thoughts, she turned and waved before pointing the camera in Penny's direction. Penny mugged and posed for a few shots, flattered by the attention, but that feeling quickly morphed into embarrassment as heat flushed her cheeks. Could Lauren tell she had been thinking about her in a way that made her pulse race and her nipples bud up? Penny shifted her posture and held her hands in front of her as if she was fending off the paparazzi.

"Come on, pretty lady!" Lauren called, playing along with the joke. "Smile for the camera."

"Get out of here," Penny protested with a laugh and peeked through her fingers. "Come sit and relax."

Lauren finally lowered her lens. "I just want to get a few more shots while I have this light."

Penny leaned back, propped up on her elbows behind her, while Lauren went back to her photography. She closed her eyes against the bright sun and let her thoughts drift back once again to that backrub. The heat of Lauren's body pressed against hers...

"Hey! Yo, Penny." A deep voice came from behind her but before she could turn to check it out, Scott from the limbo contest had plopped beside her, still wearing those thick black plastic sunglasses. Did he ever take them off? He rubbed at the backward baseball cap on his head, perfectly comfortable parked next to her, butting in on her beach time with Lauren like he belonged there.

"Hey, Scott." Penny smiled politely. It wasn't that she didn't want to hang out with him. He was a nice enough guy. It was just the thought of some alone time on the beach with Lauren sounded really good. "Where's the rest of your party?"

He took the cap off long enough to run a hand through his thick, wavy hair before returning it to its original position. "A couple of the guys are moving a little slow this morning."

"Ah." Penny's gaze flicked from his sheepish smile down to the water's edge where Lauren was still standing. Wisps of hair that had escaped from her bun were dancing on the sea breeze around her face. Illuminated by the sun at her back she looked like a Greek goddess. Penny struggled to pull herself back to the conversation with Scott. "I was hurting a little myself this morning. Damn limbo."

"It wasn't the limbo that got the best of my boys. It was the rum." He peered over the top of his glasses at Penny. "We, uh, really don't get out much."

She squinted her eyes at him in disbelief. "You guys looked like you knew your way around a party just fine last night."

"No, I'm serious." He laughed and little crinkly lines appeared around his eyes. "My brother Jason runs a tight ship. He's normally an all-work-no-play type. And we all worked for him. Duff's the only real partier in the group. He's kind of... much."

"*Worked*? Past tense?"

"Jason sold the company, and he's following his bride to the East Coast. He's moving out there right after this trip." Scott shrugged. "He's getting married and we're getting the boot."

"Well, that sucks." Penny placed her hand on his shoulder and gave it a sympathetic squeeze. If there was one thing she could relate to it was job woes. Not that she was thinking about that. "What are you going to do?"

He scooped up a handful of sand and let it slowly trickle out of his fist. He kept his eyes trained on the grains as they fell into a pile before meeting her gaze again. "I don't know. I'm enjoying this week of vacation, and I'm going to Philadelphia for my brother's wedding. After that, who knows? I'll find something. I'll worry about it then."

"I guess that's a plan." It didn't sound like much of a plan at all, but she didn't want to drag him down further by pointing that out. She had been so worried about what would happen when she returned to Vegas, but at least she knew she was returning to Vegas. She couldn't imagine surviving the kind of career free-fall Scott was living. "What kind of company did your brother own?"

"Private investigator and personal security." His mouth slid up into a lopsided grin as he flexed to show off his arm muscles. "I put these big guns to use."

"Shut up!" She punched him squarely in the showcased bicep. Did she naturally attract men in that field? "You're a bodyguard?"

He arranged his features into mock pain and rubbed at his upper arm. "I *was* a bodyguard. Now I'm just a guy on a bachelors' week."

"Hey, Dooney! Ship's about to sail." A deep voice interrupted them before Penny could apologize for pushing the issue on a sore subject.

"Ship's about to sail? Is that some kind of bodyguard code?"

"No code. Just four guys spending the day cruising the bay in a rented boat. You're welcome to join us." He flashed his big, bright, wolf-toothed smile that most likely won women over daily.

Her gaze drifted back down the beach to Lauren who was finally making her way toward their towels. *That* was how she wanted to spend her day, not boozing it up with a pack of party-guys she didn't even know. "Thanks, but I'm gonna pass this time."

He leaned in conspiratorially. "Ah. Is that your girlfriend?"

"No, not my girlfriend." What the hell was the definition of the relationship between her and Lauren? She settled on the most obvious. "Just travel companion. Although, funny story. We've actually been taking advantage of the complimentary anniversary perks the resort has been offering us, even though we're not a real couple. Hell, we only met a few days ago."

"Anniversary perks?" He raised a curious eyebrow.

"You know, free drinks, complimentary desserts…"

"Dooney!" the friend called again. "You coming or not?"

"Sorry." Scott got to his feet rather gracefully for a big guy on sand. "I've gotta run. Maybe we'll see you two at the bar later?"

"Maybe." She gave a noncommittal nod and waved as he headed off to join his friends.

Lauren walked slowly up the beach, making sure each step was steady as her feet sunk into the soft sand. She had captured a lot of good shots in the morning sun. Maybe she would take all the photos from the trip and do a show, sort of a 'rebirth of Lauren' thing. That was the kind of show the masses loved, even if it did seem a tad ridiculous to her. It was an idea, though, which was more inspiration than she'd had in quite a while.

More vacationers had set up on the beach since she and Penny had originally arrived. Lauren hadn't even noticed while she was snapping photos. That tended to happen when she got into a groove. She developed a sort of tunnel vision where the only thing that mattered was what she saw through the lens and the rest of the world just dropped away. She would never admit that out loud to anyone. It sounded so pompous and selfish, but deep down she suspected it was the way all artists felt about their craft.

That tunnel vision was probably also to blame for Lauren not noticing at first that Penny wasn't sitting alone on her towel anymore. Limbo Scott was keeping her company. He was a good-looking guy, even with his hair tucked under a cap and his eyes hidden behind cheap sunglasses. And he was a hell of a lot closer to Penny's age than she was. Lauren wasn't sure, but she guessed he was actually a few years younger than Penny. Sitting side by side on that beach towel they made quite a striking picture. Lauren raised her camera to capture the image, but quickly lowered it again. Through the lens the pair looked awkward. They were both smiling, both beautiful, but there was absolutely no chemistry in the way they interacted. No spark at all. Lauren's shoulders relaxed as Scott stood, and with a friendly wave, left Penny.

"I hope your friend didn't leave because of me." She grimaced as she approached Penny.

Penny shook her head and patted her hand on the brightly colored striped beach towel beneath her. "Not at all. He had a boat to catch. Come on, sit down and relax for a while."

Lauren did as she was told and sat. She reached for her camera bag in the shade of the resort umbrella. "Let me just tuck this away and we can get back to doing absolutely nothing but enjoying the sun and sea."

Penny pressed her fingertips against Lauren's thigh to halt her. "Actually, I was hoping you would show me the secret of taking a good picture. I mean, I don't really know how to use a camera. The only pictures I take are on my phone."

Lauren's breath caught at Penny's touch on her leg. The contact caused the same jolt through her core she had felt earlier while rubbing Penny's gorgeous back. This touch was more than just a way to get her attention. This touch was a reciprocation. It was a silent agreement. The women were leveling up from strangers who agreed to go on a trip together on a whim, pretending to be a couple, to people who were okay touching each other. "That is a crying shame. I can't even believe you would admit that to me," she teased with a wink. "Scoot closer and I'll show you the basics."

While Penny shouldered up to her, Lauren tucked the strands of loose hair that had come out of her bun behind her ear, as she prepared to take on the role of instructor.

Penny reached up and touched Lauren's earlobe. The touches were growing more intimate. "That's a pretty earring. I didn't notice you had another piercing before."

"Oh, thanks." Lauren's hand was automatically drawn straight to the tiny pearl and emerald earring in her left ear. "It was a gift from my father. After I graduated. Many years ago."

"He bought you one earring for graduation?" Penny was leaning so close, Lauren could feel her breath on her bare shoulder.

"No, smartass." Lauren smiled and set her camera on her lap in front of her. "He bought me the pair. I lost one over the years. I was heartbroken when I realized it was gone. My father's gift to me. We had gone to Cape Cod on a family vacation right after I graduated from college. I spotted the earrings in a window display at one of the cute little shops in town. My father surprised me with them the night before we left to go home."

"That's sweet." Penny's expression was fixed in a smile, but her eyes betrayed the slightest hint of sadness. The fact that Penny's relationship with her own father was strained due to recent events was not lost on Lauren. "Are you and your father still close?"

"He passed away almost ten years ago. Heart attack." Lauren paused and blew out a deep breath before continuing. "After he died, I got the extra hole and started wearing the remaining earring again. I know it's just a symbol, but it somehow makes me feel like he's still with me."

"I can understand that." Penny nodded slowly and solemnly. Of course she could understand. She knew what it was like to lose a parent as well as Lauren did.

"And it reminds me of that vacation to Cape Cod. It was the last trip we took as a family. It was special in that way." Lauren shook her head and grabbed the camera again. First the touching, then sharing personal anecdotes. Their pretend relationship was gaining speed at an alarming rate. A fake relationship was one thing, but the real deal? No, thank you.

She had been hurt far too badly by Carolyn's betrayal to want to jump into another relationship anytime soon. Even if she was spending the week in close quarters with a gorgeous, intelligent thirty-something who was currently looking at her like she held the stars and moon in the palm of her hand. She took a deep breath to calm her body's reaction to the younger woman. Best to get back to the photography lesson. "So, my number-one secret to a good pic? When you look through the lens, like this, it all comes down to perspective, the spatial relationships of the objects or people in your frame. Their sizes, the placement, the space in between them. It's the difference between your photos looking lifelike and looking totally flat. Here, you take a look."

Penny took the offered camera and held it in front of her, studying it in her hands before putting her eye up to the viewer. She aimed the camera in the direction of a boat far out in the ocean. "Okay, I get that. Perspective makes sense."

"The other thing that makes or breaks a good picture is making the subject of your photo something you care about." Lauren rested her chin on Penny's shoulder to focus on the same object in the frame. She breathed in the coconut scent of Penny's tanning oil. Another jolt and tingle in her core, this time travelling down between her legs. She swallowed hard in an effort to focus her thoughts. Her voice was a breathy whisper when she spoke. "Good pictures are all about passion."

Penny lowered the camera and turned toward Lauren. Her words came out in puffs of warmth against Lauren's cheek. "Passion. Got it."

Their lips were so close; it would be effortless for Lauren to kiss her. It seemed like Penny was giving her the green light, but that was crazy. This was a *fake* relationship. They were talking about passion in *photography*, not between them. Lauren was letting herself get carried away by the whole vacation thing. Kissing those lips would be a slippery slope that could lead to no good. There was nothing but inevitable heartbreak down that path. Had she learned *nothing* from the past year? Although, if she just leaned in a little more she would make beautiful contact...

"Good morning, ladies!" Paolo's bright and phony accented voice greeted them from behind, interrupting Lauren's thoughts before she could act on them. *He saved me.* "I have complimentary mimosas. Good thing you're getting your beach time in today. Storms are supposed to be rolling in tonight." He circled around the women until he was standing in front of them offering a tray of drinks, along with his super-white smile.

Lauren followed Penny's lead and took a glass from the tray. She had missed her chance to act on the moment before Paolo made an appearance, but she had managed to do one thing right. If Paolo was correct and the next day was going to be rainy, the spa would be packed. Lauren had already booked their massages for first thing in the morning. They could enjoy their spa time before the masses descended.

She would attend the couples massage with her friend. That's all she and Penny were—*friends*. Lauren shifted back into her own space on the towel and pushed the thought of them being anything more than that from her mind. She had to. Protecting her heart had to be her number-one priority. She sipped her champagne, nodded politely as Paolo made his exit, and focused firmly on the word echoing in her mind—*friends*.

That was all they were. So why couldn't she stop wondering what it would have been like to kiss Penny?

CHAPTER TEN

Penny sat at the bar waiting for the glasses of pinot she ordered while all around her partiers danced to Cyndi Lauper's, "She-Bop." The Jammin' Eighties theme of the nightly poolside party was a hit with the resort guests and staff alike. Penny spotted Paolo on the other side of the pool dressed like he was starring on *Miami Vice* in a white suit and pink T-shirt under it. Just when she thought the guy couldn't get any cheesier. How often did the resort host this theme party? Once a month? Once a week? Did Paolo own more than one Jammin' Eighties outfit?

She paid for her drinks just as the song switched to Irene Cara belting out "Fame," Mara's favorite eighties song. She would sing it as a pump-up before all her college theater performances. Mara would have loved the whole throwback-themed party. A twinge of guilt hit Penny at the thought of her bestie. She should have called and checked in with Mara instead of just texting her the past couple of days. It wasn't so much that she was avoiding Mara, as she was avoiding the Rothmoor. Penny couldn't bear the thought of hearing the Rothmoor was operating just fine without her. Back in Las Vegas the world was still spinning even while she vacationed. But Penny did miss Mara, and as she carefully carried the glasses of wine past the dance floor full of bright print Jams shorts and neon-colored T-shirts, she couldn't help smiling thinking of her.

Lauren shook her shoulders along to the music as she took her drink, clearly into the 80s theme herself. "I haven't heard this song in *forever*." She beamed before taking a sip of her wine. "And I feel like I haven't had a normal drink in forever either. What is it about vacation that makes you feel like you have to turn to frozen fruity drinks with zany straws? Sure they're fun and festive, but I'll take a crisp glass of pinot grigio over that any day."

"Hold up." Penny frowned, her own sweating glass of wine poised at her lips. "You're not abandoning our vacation people pledge already, are you?"

"Absolutely not. All I'm saying is you can't deny the classics."

Even while hitching her body up onto the high iron chair at their cocktail table on the edge of the dance floor, Lauren appeared graceful. It was no surprise to Penny that Lauren was a fan of the classics. Everything about her screamed class and beauty. Earlier, when Lauren had been teaching her about photography, Penny had been almost certain Lauren was going to kiss her. Or had Penny just hoped for it? She held the cool glass of wine to her cheek, hoping to relieve the sudden heat at the image of her lips pressing against Lauren's.

She had to stop thinking like that. She had to shut the feelings down. This was a friend of her mother's whom Penny was thinking about in this way. She had to stop imagining Lauren's hands on her and how it made the skin around her nipples go tight. Penny was lucky that Paolo had interrupted them earlier, before she did something foolish.

"Earth to Penny." Lauren waved a hand in front of Penny's face. "I lost you there for a second."

"Sorry." Penny blinked hard and took another sip of wine. "I was just…uh…thinking."

"Obviously." Lauren laughed and her eyes sparkled with amusement. Could she know that Penny had been fantasizing about kissing her? "I was saying, Scott and the boys just arrived. They're over there. By the bar."

"Well, I guess we shouldn't be shocked to find a bachelor party at an eighties event." Penny twisted in her seat to get a good view of the guys. "Seems fitting, right?"

"Sure. Next to arrive will be a poltergeist, then an extraterrestrial." Lauren grinned. "Seriously, if you want to hang out with them, it's fine with me."

"No." Penny faced her. "Scott's a nice guy, but I don't need to insert myself into their celebration. This is a guys' week for them."

"I'm not so sure that's how he feels about it." Lauren raised her eyebrows and sucked her bottom lip between her teeth. *Very sexy.* "Don't look now, but…"

"You came!" Scott sidled right up to their table and set his beer bottle down on the glass, making himself at home. He flashed that big toothy smile at her. "I was hoping you would."

"And you guys didn't end up lost at sea. I guess it was a good day all around."

"It would have been even better if you had come with us." He tipped his head and regarded Penny. The lost puppy dog eyes he gave her indicated that he might be more than a little tipsy. "You know, you could make up for it by hanging out with us now."

"Oh, well we *would*, but…" Penny looked to Lauren for help with her excuse, but all she got was an amused grin, a shrug, and watery eyes suggesting Lauren was choking back a laugh.

Fortunately it was Paolo to the rescue, greeting the women with a polite bow. "Excuse me, Miss Lauren, Miss Penny. I was hoping to see you here tonight."

"What do you know? We're two for two," Lauren quipped while Penny bit her cheek to keep from laughing at the absurdity of the men they were attracting to their table. "Sorry, Paolo, please go on."

"Yes ma'am." Paolo bowed again. "I wanted to let you know I signed you up to participate in the Sweetheart Sweeps competition Wednesday night."

"Sweetheart what?" Penny frowned. The limbo contest was one thing, but she had had enough competing for one week. What was this, some kind of vacation Olympics?

"Sweetheart Sweeps. It's here, poolside Wednesday night at eight. You will be competing against three other couples in a test to prove how well you know your special someone."

"How well I know my *special someone?*" Penny struggled to make sense of the words. Finally she caught Lauren's raised eyebrow stare and the pieces fell into place. "Oh! My special someone! Of course."

She and Lauren were supposed to show off how well they know each other, like the perfect couple they were pretending to be. It would be one hell of a trick. Well, the free drinks had been fun while they lasted.

"And there will be prizes, so bring your A-game, ladies." Paolo gave a sage nod before excusing himself and moving on to his next couple.

"Oh my god." Penny dissolved into giggles and buried her face in her hands the second he was out of earshot. "We are not doing this."

Lauren took a long, cool sip of her wine. "Oh, why the hell not? It will be fun."

"The guy said there would be prizes." Scott shrugged as he chimed in. He had kept so quiet while Paolo was present at their table, Penny had forgotten he was still standing there.

Penny shook her head. "We'll get trounced. We met, like, *three* days ago. I don't even know how to spell your last name."

"I doubt they're going to ask you that," Scott pointed out. "You're supposed to be a couple celebrating your anniversary. They probably assume you have the same last name."

"You're not helping the cause." Lauren placed a hand on his buff shoulder before turning back to Penny. "We can totally do this. We have almost forty-eight hours to study up."

"I don't know."

"Don't be a wimp." Lauren's eyes shone mischievously as she drummed her perfectly manicured fingertips against the glass top. "Be vacation people."

Penny rubbed at the condensation on her wineglass. She had become a real sucker for the tag line, but even knowing that, she still couldn't resist. She had a need to impress Lauren, to keep up with her. She slid her palm around the glass and raised it in a salute. "Vacation people. Bring it on."

CHAPTER ELEVEN

On the plus side, it wasn't the searing back pain from sleeping on the pullout bed that woke Penny up at three forty-two a.m. but it was, unfortunately, the eardrum splitting, high-pitched peal of the hotel fire alarm. Her pain was only confirmed as Penny rolled to the edge of the thin, crappy mattress to get out of bed. Growling, she sat up and rubbed at the small of her back.

"You have got to be kidding me." Lauren appeared in the doorway of her bedroom, disheveled from a couple hours of sleep. She held her hands over her ears, and squinted as if she was attempting to block the sound from her brain.

"Don't worry, it's most likely not an actual fire," Penny reassured in a very loud voice. She had dealt with plenty of hotel evacuations due to fire alarms being tripped for one reason or another. Panic certainly never made the process any easier. "I'm sure it's just a false alarm."

"I have no intentions of roasting like a marshmallow while we sit here waiting to find out." Lauren shook her head. "Grab something to cover yourself and let's get out of here."

Penny continued to press a hand on her back while she dug through her suitcase for a light cotton zip hoodie, then grabbed her key card, phone, and wallet from the desk.

Minutes later the women were part of the sleepy throng shuffling down the four flights of stairs to the ground floor. Penny slipped a hand into Lauren's as they descended to keep from getting separated. A shiver rushed through her body that she suspected had more to do with the contact between them than the adrenaline that had released in her system. Finally outside they followed resort staff instructions and moved to the area deemed a safe distance from the building.

"I don't see any fire. I don't even see any fire trucks." Lauren turned her head from left to right as she scanned the grounds.

"They'll come. And we're not going to be allowed back in there until they do." Penny nodded toward the building. "We're gonna be out here a while."

"So, now what?" Lauren shrugged. The white button-down shirt she had hastily thrown on nearly covered the short bottoms of her pajama set so that it looked like that was all she was wearing. Heat buzzed between Penny's legs as she gazed along the hemline of the white, gauzy fabric against Lauren's long, tanned legs.

She turned away to keep her reaction in check and surveyed their surroundings. The stairwell exit had dumped them out on the side of the hotel, a part of the resort she and Lauren had explored their first evening there. They hadn't spent much time in the area, but Penny recalled the winding path. "I have an idea. Come on."

She directed Lauren to the paved path, but paused next to an elderly couple leaning on each other at the edge of the crowd, clearly worn out from the excitement of the night. "Excuse me, we're going to be out here for a minute yet. There are benches in the gazebo right over there. You may be more comfortable sitting while you wait."

"Oh, thank you." The old woman smiled kindly before taking the advice and allowing her husband to lead her to the gazebo.

Lauren bumped Penny's shoulder. "You just can't shut it off, can you?"

"What?" Penny feigned ignorance and batted her eyelashes as they followed the path lined with lampposts. She couldn't stop the grin spreading across her face.

"You don't have to be the cruise director here. You're on *vacation*, remember?"

"Ha, ha, smartypants." Penny stuck out her tongue. "I was just trying to be nice. I can be nice *and* be on vacation."

"Maybe you should be nice to me and let me go take a seat on the benches in the gazebo instead of taking me on a midnight hike." Lauren gave Penny's upper arm a little squeeze.

Warmth started in Penny's chest and spread through her whole body. It was so easy, the back and forth between them. She hadn't felt that kind of instant connection with someone in a long time. Maybe it was because Lauren was more mature than the girls Penny used to date. Definitely more so than Cyndi who spent more time Snapchatting and picking fights with random people on social media than interacting face-to-face with her actual girlfriend. Or Danyelle whose love for video gaming all-nighters made it nearly impossible for her to hold down a job. Not that she and Lauren were *dating*. And in all fairness, Penny had been a lot younger and less mature back then too. But she liked this. Lauren was smart, sophisticated and leaning in closer and closer as they continued down the path.

"If we're gonna be outside in the middle of the night, I figure we should be comfortable." Penny smirked. Either Lauren genuinely didn't remember what waited along the path just around the bend, or she was playing along with Penny's moonlight adventure, indulging her. "We're almost there."

"Almost where?" Lauren's voice was light with laughter when she finally saw their destination. She clapped her hands, her expression reflecting her delight. "Brilliant! This is some next-level vacation people stuff."

At the side of the path were four large hammocks, each of them big enough to accommodate a couple and all of them empty. Their own private hideaway from the crowd where they could relax until the chaos dissipated.

"I thought you might like it." Pride surged through Penny at Lauren's reaction. She stretched out an arm as they approached the first hammock. "After you."

Lauren didn't wait to be asked twice. Even mounting a hammock Lauren showed grace. Her long legs swooped into the air in a pike position as she swiftly went from sitting on the edge of the net to lying down, leaving just enough room for Penny to scramble in beside her. She was like a gymnast hopping onto a trampoline. A definite ten out of ten performance.

"Come on, what are you waiting for?"

The truth was, Penny was waiting for her heartbeat to return to a normal pace. The sight of those tanned legs stretched in front of her, combined with the invitation to join Lauren in the confined space had her blood pumping. But that wasn't exactly the kind of thing Penny could just blurt out. She had to act cool. They weren't really a couple. It was all just an act. She had to remember that none of this really meant anything. Even if there wasn't anyone around to witness it, it was still just a game.

But still, the hammock had been her idea in the first place, and there was no backing out now. "Okay, let me just..." She attempted to roll her body onto it smoothly, but the result was much more like an unwieldly plop. As she sank into the net, it bobbed and bounced. Her legs tangled up with Lauren's as she struggled to get into a comfortable position. Penny closed her eyes and willed her cheeks not to blush as a wave of heat rode up her body at the contact between the two of them. She needed to chill out and get herself together. Coming to rest on her side, she found herself face-to-face with a grinning Lauren.

"Comfy?" She brushed a strand of Penny's hair to the side with a light touch of her fingertips. "So now is probably a good time to talk about what we like."

"What we...like?" Penny repeated dumbly. Her right breast was pressed against Lauren's left one. She liked *that*. But somehow she sensed that wasn't quite what Lauren meant.

"Yes. Our favorite this-or-that. Books, movies, television shows—whatever. You know, for the contest Paolo roped us into? The Sweetheart Sweeps? We need to prepare."

"Right!" Penny recovered and attempted to play it cool. "What is your favorite television show? Such a burning question. I've been meaning to ask you that for days now."

"Hmm." Lauren laughed. "*Designing Women.* Without a doubt. It's a classic sitcom with good old-fashioned eighties feminism and charm. You?"

"*Friends.*" Penny tried to ignore the tingle in her core as Lauren's knee grazed her bare thigh. Focus. *Stay on track.* "Favorite color?"

"Orange. And I already know yours." Lauren smirked. "It's black."

"It is not black," Penny protested with a laugh. "What made you say that?"

"You wear it all the time," Lauren pointed out with a semi-shrug, probably the best she could manage with gravity pulling both of them to the center of the hammock.

"That's not an indicator. Black is professional and converts easily to nightlife. It's convenient. Besides, it's not like you go around wearing orange all the time."

"I like to keep people guessing."

That was the truth. In the moment, Penny was guessing whether or not it would be appropriate to lean in and kiss Lauren's full lips. They were lying so close to one another, she could feel Lauren's breath on her cheek. Just a slight turn of her head and their mouths would make delicious contact. What would Lauren taste like? This time the tingling moved south between Penny's legs. She hoped the flimsy material of her pajama shorts didn't betray the dampness she felt down there. The wailing of sirens in the distance signaled fire trucks had finally made the scene, but there in the hammock the air was still and peaceful. They were cocooned in their own little world.

Lauren stroked a lazy finger along Penny's jawline, and their gazes locked. "Do you have any other *burning questions* for me?"

"Just one." Penny's voice was thick with desire. The touch was all the encouragement she needed to make her move. Lauren had to be feeling the connection too. As if drawn to those beautiful lips by a force she couldn't resist, Penny slowly closed the gap between them, getting closer and closer until…

"We're all clear to go back inside!" A deep male voice called from the path right as a bright beam of an official security-grade flashlight shone across them, causing them to raise an arm to shield their eyes from the light. "Come on back to your rooms. It's safe. Just a false alarm."

Penny bit her lip to keep from giggling. Probably just as well. What had she been thinking, trying to kiss Lauren? The guy just saved her from potential epic embarrassment. Acting on the moment and facing rejection would have made the rest of their vacation very uncomfortable. This wasn't a real relationship. Not in *that way*. She was getting caught up in the game.

The security guard's beam remained on them until Lauren thanked him. Then he finally moved along the path to rescue anyone else who had lost their way in the chaos. The interruption broke the spell, and once again they were just two friends who happened to be smooshed together in a hammock. Penny's cheeks burned with ridiculous shame.

Fortunately, once the guard was out of earshot, Lauren broke the awkward silence. "I guess we should get back and get a little sleep." She rolled out of the net on the far side, totally sticking her landing on solid ground while Penny attempted an equally graceful exit on her side. She let out a groan and rubbed at her lower back as she stood up. Lauren's brow wrinkled in concern. "You know, sleeping on that pullout can't be helping your back any. I have that big king-size bed. There's plenty of space. You should just sleep with me."

Sleep with her? Sleep in the same bed as Lauren? Penny's heart rate increased again. "That sounds…good. Thanks." She avoided eye contact with Lauren as she said it, hoping she sounded much more casual and cool than her pulse would reveal. Maybe she could take a quick cold shower before hitting the sheets, or maybe the walk back would give her revved-up libido a chance to chill. One way or another, she wouldn't let herself fall into the trap again. No more thinking about kissing

Lauren. They were just two women on a vacation together. This relationship stuff was all an act.

She ran the thoughts on a loop in her brain as they marched back to the hotel. Maybe if she continued to think it, it would stick.

CHAPTER TWELVE

Lauren lay facedown on the table, eyes closed, while a stern-looking woman with very strong hands rubbed, patted, and otherwise manipulated the muscles in her back. She should have felt completely relaxed, totally carefree. Instead, her body had hit Zen status, but her mind was racing with memories of the past night.

After that damn alarm had jolted her awake in the middle of the night, things had taken a curious and fascinating turn. First, Penny had led her to that secluded part of the resort with the hammocks. Lauren's body had come alive pressed against Penny's. Even reflecting on it while on the massage table, Lauren's nipples twitched in delight. She had been so certain Penny was going to kiss her. If only that guard hadn't come along with his intruding flashlight, breaking up the intimate moment! Lauren had hoped by inviting Penny into her bed they could pick up where they left off, but back in the hotel room, the mood had changed. They had simply crawled between the sheets and said goodnight.

Of course, Lauren hadn't actually fallen asleep. Instead she lay there in the dark master suite wondering where she had gone wrong. Had she imagined the impending kiss? Misread a sign?

She opened one eye and peered at Penny on the table next to hers. The new-age style music piped into the room gave the perfect soundtrack to Lauren's fantasies of caressing Penny's bare shoulders, kissing her neck.

Somehow things had shifted over the past few days and she no longer thought of the younger woman as just a travel buddy along for the adventure. Now Penny was someone she wanted to know better, someone she could find herself attached to. That was the exact reason why she should stop allowing herself these delicious daydreams of making love to Penny. She didn't need an attachment. The two of them would never work out. After the trip, Penny would go back to her busy career-driven life in Las Vegas, and Lauren had her own obligations to her art back in Chicago. It would be a relationship doomed from the start. Why choose heartbreak?

Lauren squeezed both of her eyes shut and attempted a deep, relaxing breath. She had to force the whole idea of being with Penny out of her mind. She had to be practical. She had to guard her heart. Plus, her bed invite had obviously fallen flat. She didn't want to make a fool of herself fawning all over a woman who had simply gone along with the trip to the Waverly Winds as a way to escape her own troubles. Lauren was more mature than that.

"Your shoulders are tense again," the masseuse admonished her. "What's happening here? Another deep breath. Clear your mind. Empty it out. No more thinking. Only feeling."

Lauren took the breath as instructed, but the irony wasn't lost on her. It was definitely feeling that had her in this tangle in the first place.

As part of the couple's massages, they had enjoyed brunch at the spa, which had been excellent planning on Lauren's part since the entire population of the resort seemed to be milling around the lobby area when they were done with their rubs. With the weather forecasted to be bleak all day, Lauren suspected the resort restaurants and bars would be packed for the duration. The effect of all those people piled into one place was a high volume, high humidity combination that threatened to undo any Zen she had actually managed to achieve during her time at the spa. Her instinct was to make a dash through the throng for the elevator bay, but her gaze was drawn to the picture window right outside the spa area. There was a lull in the storm, and even though the sky remained dark and dreary, the rain seemed to have taken a break.

Struck with inspiration and a desperate need to escape the crowd, Lauren hoisted her camera strap up on her shoulder and looped her other arm through Penny's. "Come on. I need some fresh air."

"You mean outside?" Penny's voice was doubtful, but she allowed Lauren to drag her out the front door of the main lobby.

"It's not raining now." She made her point by releasing her hold on Penny and stepping out from under the cover of the valet parking area. "Don't be a chicken. Get out here."

"I'm not a *chicken*." Penny laughed and stepped around the puddles of rainwater that had pooled onto the black asphalt of the drive.

Lauren already had her camera raised and was focusing in on a rain-soaked poppy in the landscaping along the driveway. "The raindrop really is one of the most beautiful natural phenomena on this planet." She snapped a few shots and fought the urge to comment on Penny's beauty as well. Just because she wasn't acting on her feelings didn't mean she couldn't capture that beauty on film. She turned her lens to Penny, who was bent over the patch of yellow flowers gently brushing her fingertips across the wet petals. The red and white swirl print of her sundress beside the flowers made a striking pop of color against the gray backdrop of the sky.

When Penny realized she had become the object of the photoshoot, she stood up straight and raised her hands in front of her in protest. "No, please! I'm probably a wreck after being at the spa."

"Shut up. You're absolutely stunning." The words were out before Lauren could stop them. To cover up her feelings, she kept talking. "Don't tell me you're not aware of that. Besides, in that dress you're quite the…picture."

"Ha, ha." Penny rolled her eyes, but she twirled and made her skirt flare before striking a pose, one hand on her hip, one on her head.

A couple of drops hit Lauren's bare arms and she looked down at the asphalt to confirm it was raining again. A glimpse of Penny's red dress in the rippling water gave her an idea. "Could you take one step to the right?"

In spite of the rain suddenly coming down harder in full, plump drops, Penny did as Lauren commanded. "Are you taking a picture of that puddle? Because it is raining again and we are getting soaked."

"This shot will be worth it, trust me," Lauren confirmed from behind her camera. "Absolutely gorgeous."

A clap of thunder made both women jump. As streaks of lightning crossed the sky, Penny gasped and grabbed her hand tightly.

Caught momentarily off guard by the contact, Lauren looped the strap of her camera over her shoulder and ran her gaze from their clasped hands, up the wet skin of Penny's arm to her face. A raindrop rested right at the edge of Penny's lip, and Lauren was struck with the urge to kiss it off. A glimpse at the way Penny's rain-soaked sundress clung to her slim, muscular frame sealed the deal. Damn it all to hell. Lauren wanted to kiss her. She locked her eyes on Penny's. Did she suspect a flash of encouragement there? It was the last push she needed. Even under the steamy heat of the day, the skin around Lauren's nipples tightened and she stepped closer, ready to make contact with Penny's full lips.

"Ladies!" Paolo's questionable accent broke across the driveway. Lauren turned to find the goofy butler with the absolute worst timing in the world rushing toward them with a giant blue and white striped golf umbrella held proudly above his head. "Don't worry, I'll get you inside and out of the storm."

"I guess we should go in." Penny's voice came out in a breathless whisper. It was impossible for Lauren to determine if the cause was the second clap of thunder that boomed around them or broken anticipation from what might have happened before Paolo's untimely appearance.

"Yes, I guess you're right." She bit her lip in an attempt to swallow down her feelings. A first kiss in the rain would have been so right. Of course there was always the chance that she had misread the hand holding. The memory of the two of them spending the night in the same bed with no results hadn't shaken from Lauren's mind quite yet. It was lurking there like a warning. Don't be a *fool.*

"Ladies." Paolo prompted them as he covered the fake couple with his umbrella and led them back into the building.

As the three of them squeezed their way through the throng of people in the lobby, Lauren's discontentment with the crowd returned full force. Judging by the scrunched-up look on Penny's face, she didn't care to be a part of the mob either. Paolo, on the other hand, appeared to be in heaven.

"Now don't let this weather get you down." His bright, white grin didn't falter for a second. "There are plenty of activities going on inside the resort. There's karaoke in the Sunset Lounge, and in Conference Room A we'll be showing that one rom-com with Drew Barrymore and Joey what's-his-name. You know, the one that was out last Christmas? It's funny. Really funny. The two of you will love it."

Lauren closed her eyes and hoped the crowd would disappear, or at the very least Paolo and his phony accent. He was still going on about Joey what's-his-name. If she didn't get away from the whole mess soon, her head might explode right there in the middle of the lobby. Paolo had interrupted her about a million times since she had arrived at the resort; it was time for her to respond in kind.

"Thank you, Paolo." She cut him off mid rom-com rave. "I'm sure we'll find a way to be entertained, but it was very sweet of you to be concerned about us."

"My pleasure, miss." Paolo excused himself with an awkward bow.

"Wow." Penny laughed and her expression lightened as she pushed a wet strand of hair off her face. "Can you get the rest of these people to bow out of here?"

"I wish," Lauren said with a sigh. The chilled air inside the resort along with the dampness on her skin was giving her a case of the goose pimples. She was more than ready to get out of her wet clothes. "No interest in karaoke or rom-coms?"

Penny pulled a face and shook her head. "I'm not much of a rom-com gal. And the thought of drunk Scott and the gang following us around all day makes me want to scream. I'd rather sit in the hotel room all day and do nothing."

"Well, *that* doesn't sound very fun." Lauren's gaze scanned the lobby area before coming to rest on the gift shop. "But don't worry. I have an idea."

Thirty minutes later they were back in their pajamas, parked on the king-size bed and Penny could not have been happier. From the moment Lauren suggested a movie and wine day in the seclusion of their own room Penny had been on board. A quiet day in with Lauren beat the hell out of drunken frat boy karaoke any day, even if the women *were* just travel companions. Plus, as Lauren had pointed out when she proposed the plan, they could use the time to study up on each other for the upcoming contest their dear friend Paolo had signed them up for.

Penny topped off their wineglasses while Lauren queued up the film.

"You nixed the rom-com, so I picked something else." Lauren poked at the keyboard on the laptop, navigating her desktop. "*Desert Hearts*. Classic lesbian drama from the eighties. It's a must see."

"A must see," Penny repeated dumbly between sips of white wine. Something on the computer caught her attention and she waved her hand frantically to halt Lauren from clicking any further. "Wait, go back."

Lauren paused, her long fingers poised over the keyboard. "Go back to what?"

"That file on your desktop that said Stormy Day Pics. Is that from today?"

Lauren minimized the movie queue window and clicked on the camera icon that appeared in the lower right corner. "I just quickly downloaded them when we got back to the room. I haven't even looked at them myself."

Penny scooted closer to the computer screen. "Now is as good a time as any. Let's take a peek."

"You're nosy," Lauren teased, but she opened up the file anyway. Both of their moods had lifted significantly since they left the crowd of the lobby behind.

"Yes, I am. Oh, wow." The first image filled the screen. It was a close shot of a bright yellow poppy in such crisp focus that anticipation of the raindrop teetering on its petal falling actually stirred in Penny's chest. "That's...amazing."

"Nature did all the heavy lifting with that one, but thank you." Lauren appeared pleased with the compliment in spite of her statement.

How did she find beauty on such a bleak day? She was amazed how Lauren had captured the details of life all around her that Penny had missed in the moment. She laughed out loud when they came to the series of photos of her twirling her skirt and then mugging for the camera. Penny covered her face with her hands, embarrassed by her reaction. "I'm clearly an attention whore."

"Gorgeous is what you are." Lauren's voice was nearly a whisper, causing Penny to peek out from between her fingers and look at the screen once more.

"Oh!" Penny gasped at the image on the computer. It was her in the red dress reflected in the ripples of a puddle on the asphalt and the effect was absolutely enchanting.

"I know." Lauren inched closer to her on the bed and reached up to tuck a stray strand of hair from Penny's messy bun back behind her ear. "I couldn't resist you."

Penny swallowed hard, partly because of pride, but mostly because of what she heard in Lauren's voice. Despite all the near misses in the past two days, there was no mistaking the desire behind her words. Could Lauren have been feeling the same pull of attraction? A rush of excitement tickled in her middle, followed by a pulse of heat that quickly traveled south from there. Crossing that line from friends to lovers would change the whole dynamic of the trip. It *could* just be a vacation fling. People did that sort of thing all the time. She could enjoy this time with Lauren, and it didn't have to have some deep, involved meaning. *Vacation people. Let go.* She locked her gaze on Lauren, just to be sure. "Are you saying that—"

"I'm saying that I've been wanting to do this for days." Lauren leaned in before Penny could finish her thought and kissed her hard and purposefully on the mouth.

As soon as their lips made contact, Penny knew it was right. Her tongue slid against Lauren's, sending another shiver through her body. She was finally kissing Lauren Hansen after thinking about it for days. And it was so much more incredible than she had fantasized. After fighting her urges for all this time, she was desperate to be close. Her pussy twitched with anticipation as Lauren worked her hands under the silk of her pajama top. In one swift movement, Lauren pulled it up over Penny's head and discarded it on the side of the bed. Penny's exposed nipples went hard. Lauren laid her back against the pillows and greedily sucked one nipple between her lips. Penny gasped and her pussy clenched again with want.

"God, yes." She tangled her hands in Lauren's hair, encouraging the licks and sucks on her breast. The edges of reality went fuzzy as Penny dropped her head back and relished the touch of Lauren's magical mouth on her skin. Lauren nibbled and teased with precisely the right amount of teeth raking against her taut nipples. When Penny thought she could take no more, she put her hands on Lauren's shoulders, encouraging her to apply that mouth a little lower. The teasing suddenly came to a halt. Penny opened her eyes, completely prepared to beg for more, but Lauren stopped her before she could actually form the words.

"Take off your panties."

Penny quickly hooked her thumbs in the waistband of her boy shorts and pulled them down over her hips. She would do any damn thing Lauren wanted if it meant she could have more time with those beautiful lips against her skin. She flung the shorts over the side of the bed with a flourish and reached for the edge of Lauren's tank top. She managed to tug it off as Lauren lowered herself onto her again.

Their bare breasts pressed together—skin on skin—and Lauren worked her knee between Penny's thighs. She applied her mouth to Penny's neck and licked a trail down to her collarbone. Once again Penny found that words escaped her, and nothing but a lustful moan passed her lips. Then Lauren reached down to her pussy, teasing her with a feather touch. Penny turned to total jelly.

"You're so wet." Lauren's husky voice came out in breathless bursts.

"I'm wet because I want you." Penny grabbed Lauren's hand and pressed it firmly against her clit.

Lauren ran her fingers over the hard bud, making swift rhythmic circles before inching down and positioning herself between Penny's legs. She planted a light kiss on Penny's heat and wiggled out of her own pajama bottoms, keeping eye contact the whole time.

Penny squirmed, craving Lauren's touch. A smile played at Lauren's lips as she lowered her face against Penny's pussy. Lauren exhaled against Penny, making her clit pulse with anticipation. She felt a swelling within her, a wave she fought to hold back. Her hips bucked as Lauren's tongue pressed against her once…twice…a third long lap curled around her clit and Penny clutched at the sheets and closed her eyes. Bursts of color blossomed against the insides of her eyelids like acid trip flower patterns in a kaleidoscope. Her body shuddered and shook as the orgasm rocked through her.

"That was…amazing."

Lauren grinned, but only gave her a brief moment to catch her breath before topping her with a kiss on the mouth. She moaned against Penny's lips. "You're sexy as hell when you come undone. I want to see you do it again."

She hitched her knee along Penny's side and pressed her slick heat against Penny's sensitive clit. She kept her gaze locked on Penny's face as she gracefully rolled her hips, grinding against Penny.

Penny swallowed hard as she felt herself teetering on the edge once more. The sensation came on fast and furious as she moved along with Lauren riding the swell. She bit her lip in an attempt to hold back. She had never come from tribbing. It had been a long time since she had been with a woman, but there *had* been other women. Somehow everything with Lauren felt fresh and new—like her first time all over again, only with much more skill. That was the beauty of sleeping with an older woman. Lauren sure as fuck knew what she was doing.

Their bodies fit against each other perfectly and the ensuing pressure and friction was heavenly. Penny felt the pleasure building as the dam threatened to burst.

"Yes...Lauren...fuck me," Penny growled. Her hips rocked along with Lauren's, their pussies between them slick with their juices. Finally she gave in to the orgasm and pleasure rocked her, a series of electric pulses rushing through her as she came.

Lauren cried out as she peaked too. She arched her back and gave one last roll of the hips before collapsing onto the bed, glowing with sweat, and for the moment, apparently sated.

Penny nuzzled into the warmth of Lauren's long body and sighed contentedly. She had let go of control and allowed herself to go with the flow, sliding right down that slippery slope to paradise. Her body buzzed; her heart pounded. Through her post-orgasmic haze, one thing was crystal clear to her. She was hooked on Lauren's magic and she wanted more of it.

CHAPTER THIRTEEN

Lauren sat on the edge of the bed and pulled her silky robe onto her shoulders. She didn't want to leave Penny alone after what they had shared, but she hadn't been able to fall asleep. Not wanting to disturb Penny, she moved her fidgeting self to the living room.

Penny. The silently slumbering beauty wrapped in the silky sheets in the master suite. Lauren still couldn't believe how the afternoon had snowballed from looking at pictures to, well, *that*. She took another long look at her as she left the room. Penny sighed in her sleep and looked as peaceful and satiated as Lauren felt.

Lauren shut the door to the master bedroom behind her as quietly as possible and tiptoed across the room. She tugged her robe tightly around her. It was an emerald-green, lace-edged wraparound that Carolyn had given her a couple of Christmases ago. Lauren had always loved the way she looked in that robe—the way the bright jewel-tone contrasted with her skin, the way it brought out the green of her eyes. But now, standing in the middle of a hotel room hundreds of miles away from the home she had shared with Carolyn, her body still buzzing with the afterglow of several intense orgasms, Lauren thought it was time to do a major overhaul of her possessions. There was no sense holding on to things that reminded her of Carolyn and the life they had shared. That life was gone. Lauren was beyond ready for a fresh start.

A half-empty bottle of wine sat on the desk and Lauren smiled, remembering how quickly they had gone through the first one when they came in from the maddening crowd of the lobby. She considered pouring herself another glass, but with dinner less than two hours away, she decided coffee was the better choice. Dropping a pod of Columbian into the device, she used the brewing time to check her phone. She was surprised to see a text from James. *VENUE ISSUE. TEXT ME.*

It was time stamped two hours earlier. Poor James was probably freaking out while Lauren was distracted by…enjoying her vacation. She dialed him up with one hand while she stirred sugar into her mug with the other. She was settling into the striped, wingback chair in the corner of the room as he picked up the call.

"Oh my god, Lauren, I'm so sorry to bother you. But also, where the hell have you been? Is there terrible phone reception there or something?" His words tumbled out across the line with his usual high-energy rush.

"James, it's fine. I just didn't hear my phone over the…" Lauren bit back a smile and reined in her racing thoughts of sex with Penny. "Nap. I was napping."

"You sound weird. What's wrong with you?" His frown carried through the line. He was an art student at Columbia College Chicago and had been Lauren's assistant for almost a year and a half. He was efficient, reliable, and very good at reading her mood. In this case, maybe too good. "Oh my god, you've found some hotsy-totsy vacation fling!"

"No!" Lauren protested, nearly spilling coffee down her robe. "I was asleep!"

"You were not asleep. You found yourself a little vacation honey."

"It's not like that at all." Her hackles rose. "You don't need to make her sound like some two-bit floozie I picked up at the Gas 'N' Go."

"I *knew* it!" His tone was victorious. "So, who's the girl?"

Although Lauren didn't like him making Penny sound like a cheap one-off, she wasn't exactly ready to 'fess up to the situation entirely either. She and James had discussed many things while working together, and they had always been very honest with one another, but she wasn't ready to spill her guts on this one. She wasn't fooling herself about the situation with Penny. If this all went up in smoke, she would hate having to eat crow about it with James. Better to error on the side of caution. She hadn't told him about her ulterior motive for spending the night in Vegas, so he wouldn't have any reason to suspect she had taken Penny along on the trip. She could still shrug the whole thing off and change the subject.

"James, let's focus here." She adopted as much of an in-charge business tone as she could muster while wrapped in silk and coming down from the high of awesome sex. "Your text said there was a venue issue with the show. What's happening?"

"Oh, right." His disappointment in missing out on the scoop was apparent, but he snapped right back into assistant mode. "A pipe burst in the basement of the Hagan. They have no water and it's going to be at least a week until the damage can be repaired."

"*At least a week?* My show opens next Thursday!" Her voice rose to a near shriek. Remembering Penny slumbering in the other room, she took a deep breath to calm herself. "James, that's one week away. What are we going to do? Postpone?"

"Well, for one, we're not going to panic. Let me check around and see what else is available. The Hagan isn't the only game in town."

The Hagan *wasn't* the only game in town. There were galleries and studios up and down the strip that served as Chicago's art district. But the location wasn't random. When they planned the show, Lauren had selected the Hagan for its reputation and its particular aesthetics. She wanted the Hagan.

"I don't know."

"Just give me until the end of the week. You enjoy your vacation and I'll sort this out. Who knows? Maybe the Hagan will be up and running earlier than expected."

It was possible the Hagan had overshot its estimation on the repairs so that everyone could be delighted when they were done sooner than expected. But doubt had already made itself at home in Lauren's mind, and her heart sank a little at the prospect of having to relocate the show. This was something James could handle, though, and there was no sense in her worrying about it until he had some facts for her. She would have to let him run with it for now.

"Okay." She sighed, resigned to let him take care of it. "End of the week. Let me know what you find out."

They said their goodbyes and clicked off the call. She tipped her head back to rest on the high back of the chair. Suddenly she wished she had gone for the glass of wine instead of coffee. She tried another one of those deep breaths, not unlike the ones she used to calm herself at the spa. She trusted James. Her show was in good hands.

Maybe she should have come clean to him about Penny. It would be fun to have someone to talk to about what happened, someone to help her sort out her feelings. He was always a good sounding board. But the distance between Las Vegas and Chicago made the whole situation with Penny so damn complicated. There wasn't even any point to overanalyzing it. Lauren didn't need complicated, especially now that things with her show had bumped up to worrisome. It was best that she just enjoy the rest of the trip with Penny. She should be more like the vacation people mantra she had been chanting to Penny all week. It was time for Lauren to take a page from her own book. Enjoy vacation, and the two of them would go back to their separate lives when the week was done.

She was still staring blankly at the ceiling, mulling it all over when Penny finally emerged from the bedroom. She snapped back to attention as Penny stretched her arms over her head and yawned.

"I can't believe I totally fell asleep like that." Penny had put her tank top and thong back on, but her movement revealed a peek at her abs between the two. "I feel like a million bucks!"

Despite her bedhead, Penny did indeed look like a million bucks. Her eyes were bright and she looked completely refreshed. She hadn't looked that relaxed since Lauren had met her back at the Rothmoor in Vegas. Maybe a good lay and a nap was all the woman needed to hit restart on her life. Maybe all Lauren really was to Penny was that good lay. It was all very vacation people of her. None of it needed to be so complicated. They were on a vacation. She would just roll with the punches and enjoy it while it lasted.

Lauren got to her feet and picked up her coffee cup from the desk. "Well, good. You're all rested up for dinner then. Don't forget. Our reservation is at seven."

"Perfect." Penny grinned at her. "I'm starving. I guess I really worked up an appetite earlier."

Exactly. Sex was another normal human need like sleep and food and air to breathe. It didn't have to be any more complicated than any of that.

"Far be it for me to keep a hungry woman waiting." Lauren sauntered across the room, not even bothering to right her robe when it slipped off her shoulder. "I'm going to hop in the shower and get myself ready."

Penny tugged at the bottom hem of her tank top as she walked toward the mini-fridge. Since she left the warmth of the king-size, the air conditioning had given her a chill. She should have put on something else when she got up, but instead she elected to parade around in her tank and panties hoping to lure Lauren into Round Two in the master suite. That had been an epic fail.

She grabbed a bottle of water from the mini-fridge, too thirsty to care that it was a seven-dollar beverage at the Waverly Winds Resort. After a day of wine and sex, she needed to hydrate. Hell, the sex was so good she should probably be replenishing electrolytes to recover. She would have to remember to offer to reimburse Lauren for the bottle of water, as well as the twelve-dollar bag of macadamia nuts she had eaten earlier. Lauren certainly carried herself with the class and style of someone who didn't worry about spending money, but Penny didn't want to just assume she was fine with loose spending on ridiculously priced snacks. After all, she had footed the bill for their stay at the resort. The least Penny could do was ante up for refreshments.

She picked up her phone as she crossed the room and plopped on the sofa. Her shoulders slumped as a dejected sigh escaped her lips. She had expected a much different reaction from Lauren when she had come out of the bedroom half-naked. Was her ass not as tempting as she believed it to be? Did she suck at the art of seduction? That couldn't be it.

Suddenly she was overwhelmed with a yearning to be with her friends. One of the pluses of rarely leaving Las Vegas because she needed to be near the casino was always having a friend within "grab a quick coffee" reach at all times. She longed to be at Café Gato, their favorite hangout, with the girls mulling over this Lauren situation. Her friends would know what she should do, or if they didn't, they'd at least find a good reason to laugh about it all.

But Vegas was far away, and a phone call to her best friend Mara would have to suffice. Mara picked up the call right away and Penny got her up to speed on her travel adventure, just like they were gossiping at the Gato.

"So you had mega-hot sex, took a nap, and then tried to drum up another go with her? You sly dog!" Penny could hear her tapping her fingertips against her lips over the phone line. It was her go-to thinking face. "But she ignored your advances. Interesting."

"And the worst part of all of this is…" Penny lowered her voice to a conspiratorial whisper, "I think I'm really falling for her."

"Oh my god." Her whisper had a faux "clutch-your-pearls" scandalous tone. "You *like her*, like her?"

"Mara." Penny sighed. "I'm serious. She's intelligent and sophisticated, and you should see the photos she takes. It's like she has art super powers. She's amazing."

"Okay, so you're really into her." Mara's tone sobered. "Did you do one of your *pros and cons* lists like you usually do about things?"

"No."

"Pie chart?"

"No." She chewed her bottom lip, hesitant to even ask her question. Her life had felt so upside down since she walked out of the casino Friday. "Am I losing my mind, or what?"

"Well, this call to me officially qualifies as checks and balances. So while your behavior is a little deviant from the norm, I wouldn't say you've reached *lost your mind* status yet."

"But I shouldn't have slept with her."

"Hell, I didn't say that." Mara was silent for a beat, as if considering the situation. "In fact, I'm proud of you."

"You're *proud* that I got it on with a woman I barely know but went on a vacation with?" Penny snorted and hoped the seven-dollar water didn't come out of her nose.

"Yep. You stepped out of your comfort zone by even going on that trip. Last-minute decision, travel companion you hardly know. You have beaten your over-analyzing brain at its own game, my friend. Maybe you should have taken time off work a long time ago."

The confidence ballooning and bolstering Penny's ego at her recent accomplishment at overcoming her inner defenses deflated as the last of Mara's words set in. She didn't *take time off* from work. She was *given* it. Why didn't anyone seem to get that? Of course, Penny wasn't supposed to talk or even think about work during the trip. She had promised Lauren. She stuck instead with the issue at hand. "But I just totally put myself out there again and she shut me down. Maybe this was all a big mistake."

"Pen, walking past a woman you've just had sex with bare-assed is hardly putting yourself out there. And besides, you do have legit dinner reservations in a bit. Stop overthinking this and enjoy your damn vacation. Go with the flow."

"Go with the flow. Go with the flow," Penny chanted as if hypnotizing herself into action. The phrase didn't feel right in her mouth, like it didn't fit—a mouthful of marbles sensation that seemed like tripping over her tongue. "I don't know. I'll try."

"Don't try. Do. Enjoy your dinner date and call me again soon." Mara's voice softened. "I miss you."

"It's not a...." Penny cut her protest short. Arguing about whether or not dinner was a date was not going with the flow, and she was determined to do her damnedest to take her friend's advice. "I miss you too."

She ended the call and drained the last of the water from her bottle in one long swallow. If she was going with the flow and having a dinner date with Lauren, then she was damn well going to make it count. She would start by dressing drop-dead gorgeous for the occasion. At least she could control that.

CHAPTER FOURTEEN

By the time the women stepped out of the elevator and back onto the main floor of the resort, the mad, muggy rush of the morning had dissipated completely. The scene in the lobby of the Waverly Winds was once again one of class and calm. Penny assumed the change was due mainly to the rowdy day drinkers returning to their rooms to 'sleep it off' before returning to enjoy the nightlife.

Lauren offered Penny her arm as they made their way down the marble hallway that led to Sawyer's Iron, the high-end steak house at the Waverly Winds. The bag of nuts Penny had eaten earlier had not quite been enough to carry her through the day, and she couldn't get the thought of ordering a big, juicy filet mignon out of her mind. A big slab of beef was appallingly contrary to her usual salad as a meal, but she had burned enough calories earlier to make up for it. Besides, she was *going with the flow*, and if her body was craving red meat, so be it. Regular life rules, be damned! She could do this.

Penny's red patent leather stilettos clicked lightly as they followed the maître d'. She gripped Lauren's arm a little tighter to help her keep her footing. Funny that her knees were still weak and wobbly from sex three hours earlier. That was the kind of thing a good orgasm could do to a woman.

Their table was secluded in the far corner of the restaurant. Floor-to-ceiling windows offered a breathtaking view of the ocean, and with the storm gone, the sunset took center stage. Penny settled into her chair and blinked. The glow of the single candle on the table danced across her lashes. The table was tiny, the setting intimate. They couldn't have been seated in a more romantic spot.

She sucked her breath in through her teeth, an attempt to calm her nerves. She hoped her smile looked less shaky than it felt. Her fingers twitched and she balled them into fists to quell it. She had fallen victim to the ambience and her nerves had kicked into high gear. She was supposed to be going with the flow like Mara advised, not freaking out because she was having what appeared to be a romantic dinner with the woman she'd just slept with.

"Is everything okay?" Lauren's lips curved into a grin. The reflection of candlelight flickered in her warm amber eyes. She didn't wait for an answer. "How about I order some wine? Is red good?"

"Red would be perfect." Penny's shoulders relaxed a pinch as Lauren took the lead. She took a couple more deep breaths to encourage the release while the bottle was ordered.

She'd had dinner with sophisticated, beautiful women before. This was no different. They'd had sex earlier, so what? It didn't mean she had to start feeling all sappy about Lauren. And just because she was completely entranced by the way Lauren's cherry red lips moved when she spoke was no reason for her brain to turn to Jell-O and her heart to go all mushy.

"Penny?" Lauren's voice had a slight edge that snapped Penny back to full focus.

Her brain *had* turned to Jell-O. She hadn't registered word one of what Lauren had been saying.

"I'm so sorry." Penny shook her head trying to clear it. "I zoned out for a minute there. It's all this relaxing and vacationing. I'm not used to it. Taking a nap is totally unheard of for me. I think it's thrown me off."

"That's what I was saying." Lauren's expression was soft, and her sweet smile reached her eyes. Her voice was silky smooth and soothing. "I know you're not happy to have this time off work, but I think it's good for you in a lot of ways that you may not have considered." She bit her lip and tilted her head as she regarded her. "Also, I'm glad you're here with me."

Penny's cheeks went warm at Lauren's confession. There was a connection between them. She hadn't imagined it. And she had to admit Lauren had a point. She hadn't given a hell of a lot of thought to work in the past twenty-four hours. Her mind had been much too occupied navigating the roller coaster of emotions spending the day with Lauren had stirred. Maybe that was all relaxing really was: keeping your mind off its usual concerns by distracting it with something else—like sex with a deliciously gorgeous woman that you had no business bedding.

"Maybe I needed a break from work," she admitted and busied her hands setting her napkin politely in her lap. Once it was in place, she rubbed the hem between her thumb and pointer finger as she talked. "This has been a banner day for me as far as taking it easy goes."

"I'm glad to hear it." Lauren paused while the waiter brought the bottle of wine to their table and poured them each a glass. When he finally left them, excusing himself with a curt bow, she continued. She raised her glass. "To a beautiful evening with a beautiful lady."

Heat rushed to her cheeks again as Penny grabbed her glass to match the gesture. The mischievous upward curl of the left side of Lauren's sexy smile sent a shiver down her spine. Lauren locked her gaze squarely on Penny's eyes. It was as if she was holding her down with the eye contact. Being held down by Lauren was a very interesting proposition. "Hear, hear," she said with a wink she regretted immediately. She hid in a sip of her wine. Her coolness was declining rapidly.

"I like that enthusiasm." Lauren raised an elegant eyebrow. "It could come in handy later."

Any last scrap of Penny's calm and cool demeanor went out the door. Heat soared straight down her body and pooled between her legs. Unfortunately, the sudden shot of electricity to her pussy at Lauren's suggestion also caused her shoulders to clench again, which caused her arm to jerk, which caused her hand to brush against the edge of the crystal wine goblet, causing a full six ounces of red wine to spill onto Penny's dress.

"Oh!" She pushed back in her chair, reflexively grabbing the napkin from her lap and dabbing maniacally at the wetness on her Greek goddess wrap dress. The red wine looked like a bloodstain as it spread across the sky-blue fabric. There was no way it would ever come out once it set in. Anyway, she couldn't just sit back down to dinner looking like a murder victim. "Excuse me, I'm going to the ladies' room to take care of this."

Lauren nodded in acknowledgment and Penny rushed as best she could without drawing any more attention to herself to the bar area where the restrooms were located. She was still clutching the white linen napkin to her midsection as she pushed through the large oak door.

The women's lounge was a peaceful haven with peach walls and a pastel floral wallpaper border that circled the room at waist level, just above the whitewashed wainscoting. It was quite the contrast from the oak-paneled bar she had passed with wall-mounted animal heads and burgundy leather upholstered chairs. Most of Sawyer's Iron was a real man's place. The ladies' room was an oasis from the overdone theme. Penny pushed through a second door on the far side of the lounge to finally reach the sinks. She avoided the mirror as she soaked the napkin under the running water. When it was saturated, she applied it to the rosy blotch on the silky fabric. It was bad enough she had ruined a perfectly good dress, but doing so by looking like a klutz in front of Lauren was too humiliating. As she blotted the stain that appeared to worsen as water slopped and splashed down the front of her dress, she mentally berated herself.

So much for appearing elegant and self-assured. So much for impressing Lauren. It was silly of her to try so hard anyway—

the result of some serious overthinking. She had spent nearly every waking moment of the past seventy-two hours with this woman and they had gotten along famously. They had been having a damn good time. So why the hell did she feel such a need to know Lauren was into her?

The dripping from the hem of her dress to her feet pulled her attention back to the moment and the incredible amount of water she had managed to slosh down the front of her dress. She tossed the sopping napkin onto the sink and frantically grabbed a handful of the thick paper hand towels from the basket on the countertop. She dabbed at the liquid over and over, but the battle was a losing one. The damage had been done. The luxurious blue fabric clung to her body with no plans to dry out anytime soon.

Surrendering to her fate, she finally raised her gaze to meet her reflection in the wall-length mirror in front of her. She looked like the same Penelope Rothmoor who had left Vegas three days earlier, but mentally she was far from the calm, cool manager who had left the casino. She was a soaking wet mess of a woman who was, most certainly, not going with the flow. Professionally, nothing could shake her. But without her job keeping her afloat she was a train-wreck. She couldn't even navigate a vacation without losing it. A *freaking* vacation.

"Penny? Are you in here?"

Lauren's muffled voice from the ladies' lounge was punctuated by the slamming of the big oak door behind her. A few more steps and she would witness the sad state of affairs that was now Penny.

The prickling at the back of her eyes was both sudden and severe, and much to her chagrin, tears slid down her cheeks before she could even try to hold them back. The absolute topper to the disaster of a date.

Lauren burst through the door using her hip to push it open. Her hands were full with their purses. "Oh my god. What's wrong? Why are you crying?"

"I'm not a go-with-the-flow person," Penny managed to choke out between sobs.

"Not in that wet dress you're not."

"I'm serious. I don't go with the flow. I'm not a vacation person. I'm completely incapable of doing this. I'm organized. I plan. I stay the course. I'm just me, and I don't think I can change that."

"Oh, Penny." Lauren deposited the handbags on the countertop and pulled Penny into her arms. "I never meant for you to change who you are. I just wanted you to relax and have fun and not stress."

Penny swiped a thumb under one eye and then the other, praying that her eye makeup hadn't been completely ruined. "I can't help that I stress about things. I stress about work. I stress about my wardrobe. I stress about my friends. And now that I'm away from all that I'm… I'm stressed about what it meant that we had sex today."

At that last part Lauren pulled back from their embrace, her long-lashed eyes went wide, and her perfect cherry lips formed an O. Her gaze searched Penny's face for a moment before she finally spoke. "Okay. I think maybe we should sit down for this conversation." She took Penny's hand in hers, grabbed their handbags from the counter, and led the way back into the lounge where they settled onto a wicker couch that had cushions with the same pattern as the ones in the main lobby of the resort.

Penny sat but continued to blot her dress with a paper towel. Her cheeks were hot with shame that she had blurted out her concerns with no filter. Maybe they could just dry her dress instead of talking about it.

Lauren wasn't falling for it. "Hey." She ran her finger along Penny's jaw, tipping her chin up and forcing Penny to meet her gaze. "Don't hide from me now. Let's talk it out."

"I'm sorry."

"You have absolutely nothing to be sorry about." Lauren shook her head. "I would find it much more disturbing if you had no feelings about what happened between us earlier."

Something in Lauren's words ticked at the back of her brain. "Wait. *Much more disturbing?* You think it's disturbing that I have feelings?" She buried her face in her hands. "I am *so* embarrassed."

"Please don't be." Lauren moved her hand to Penny's thigh and gently gave it a squeeze. "That wasn't what I meant at all. I have some feelings about it too. The only disturbing thing is what you've managed to do to this dress."

Penny shot an exasperated look at Lauren. When she saw her literally biting her lip to keep from bursting with laughter, she couldn't help but smile back.

"Penny, I like you. A lot. And this afternoon was incredible." Her brown eyes remained trained on Penny's while she spoke. "I haven't felt a connection with someone like that since... Well, let's just say I don't usually connect with people like that. We've known each other four days and in some ways it feels like a lifetime. But I think we have to be practical about this."

Practical. That was a buzzkill of a term, but it did appeal to Penny's sensibilities. "I like you too. And I think I get what you're saying."

Lauren's expression softened and she slid her hand around Penny's, weaving their fingers together. "Let's face it, neither of us is exactly ready for a relationship. We're both still healing our broken hearts. Even if that wasn't the case, I have my job and life in Chicago and yours is in Las Vegas. And Lord knows you have your hands full with that."

"We're not very practical." Penny concluded her thought with a sigh. Matters that swayed the heart rarely were.

"No, we're not. But, that said, we have the rest of the week together. There's no reason we can't enjoy being together while it lasts."

Enjoying the week together sounded pretty damn good to Penny. In fact, she recalled several good reasons Lauren had given her earlier that very afternoon for why it was a wonderful plan for the remainder of the trip. She smiled and squeezed her hand for emphasis. "I'd like that."

"It's not too go with the flow for you?"

Penny blew out a deep breath and let go of the stress that had plagued her all evening. Knowing where Lauren stood—just knowing they were in agreement on where they were going with this...whatever it was they were doing for the rest of the week, made all the difference for her. "Not at all."

"Good." Lauren rose from the couch and pulled Penny to her feet as well. "Now let's get you upstairs and out of this dress." The twitch in her lips hinted that she had more in mind than simply getting Penny into her PJs.

The lustful look Lauren fixed on her made Penny's core buzz and her pussy clench. It was all the encouragement she needed to follow her lead.

CHAPTER FIFTEEN

Lauren stood by the glass door that led to the balcony and pinched the bridge of her nose. She resisted the urge to stomp her feet like a toddler throwing a tantrum right there in the middle of her hotel room. "James, what happened to 'give it until the end of the week?'"

"Yeah, sorry about that. The good news is, I'm so damn good that it only took me twenty-four hours to realize there is nowhere available on such short notice that could possibly do our show justice."

Down below the resort window the waves crashed on the edge of the shore, then receded to their depths. Crash and retreat, over and over, shaping the sand with each motion. Making a change with every sweep that was obvious and yet irrelevant. *Imagine being such a force of nature, but having your work never truly completed.* She couldn't settle for less than the full impact her photos could have on her patrons. The venue for the show had to be spot-on. James was right. "So, what's Plan B?"

The hesitation on the other end of the line wasn't reassuring. "I guess we wait and see if the Hagan makes good on their original statement of being ready in a week. Maybe this will still work out."

"James, the word maybe isn't one I like to hear when it comes to my livelihood." She sucked in a deep breath, collecting herself. This wasn't his fault at all. For three solid weeks before she left for vacation he had worked by her side to make sure lighting, layout, and spacing was just right at the Hagan. The show was important to him too. There was nothing to be done but hope for the best and have faith that if anything came up, he would be on top of it. "But you're right. Our hands are tied until we hear back from the Hagan. Just promise me you'll keep me up to speed on any developments."

"Absolutely," he said solemnly. "And *you* promise *me* you're going to continue to enjoy your vacation, including that beach bunny spring fling you're hopping around with."

"It's not at all like that."

"Uh-huh. Bye!" he sang out before clicking off the call.

When the kid caught a whiff of something juicy, he did not let it go. She'd give him that much. The waiting to see was going to kill her. She much preferred to face things head-on, like the night before with Penny all tripped out and nervous in the bathroom instead of just asking Lauren point-blank what was happening between them. Maybe that kind of wisdom and self-assurance came with age. Lauren couldn't imagine that Penny backed down from anything at her job at the Rothmoor Casino. Of course, when it came to affairs of the heart, things were always a bit stickier.

They had come back to the room after their talk and picked up where they had left off that afternoon. If the night they had shared tangled up in the bed of the master suite had been any indication of how the rest of their stay at the Waverly Winds was going to go, they were in for a scorching hot couple of days together while this paradise lasted. After all of the preaching she had done to Penny about being vacation people, Lauren couldn't let her work worries stand in her way of making the most of their time. James had been right about that too.

As if on cue, Penny came bouncing out of the master suite dressed and ready for fun in the sun on the beach. Lauren was still wrapped in her old robe she had put on after getting out of bed that morning.

Penny had moved her suitcase and belongings into the bedroom at some point the night before, establishing a definite shift in the mood of the vacation as far as their situation went. They were no longer two strangers who ended up on a vacation together under crazy circumstances. They were lovers.

Penny paused midstride when she saw Lauren's expression. "What's wrong?"

"Nothing." Lauren plastered a smile on her face. "Nothing's wrong."

"Mmmm." Penny furrowed her brow. She closed the distance between them and wrapped her arms around Lauren from behind and peppered Lauren's neck with kisses. "I've seen your, 'everything is totally right' face, and this is not it. Talk to me."

The contact of Penny's lips on her skin had an immediate effect on Lauren. Her shoulders unclenched, her mouth eased into a genuine smile, and a tingle of excitement slithered down her spine, which made her nipples go rock hard. "Okay, you're right. I just got off the phone with my assistant. We might have to postpone the show."

Penny spun her around. "What do you mean? Is there something we can do?"

She shook her head. "There's a problem with the venue and we just have to wait it out." She threw her hands up in surrender. "There's nothing I can do right now."

"You're sure about that? I'll help anyway I can."

"You're very sweet and I appreciate that very much, but I'm sure. It's a waiting game at this point."

"I know something that would take your mind off that," Penny purred.

Heat pulsed between Lauren's legs and she planted a kiss on Penny's forehead. "I like where this is going."

"Not that." Penny giggled and pulled back, still holding her hand. "There will be plenty of time for that tonight, *after our victory.*"

"Sweetheart Sweeps! It's tonight. How could I have forgotten?" Lauren had been so distracted, first by their evening out and then by James's phone call that the upcoming competition had completely slipped her mind. They weren't exactly a couple, but they were much more together than they had been when they agreed to the whole thing. Still, victory would be a hell of a stretch. "Are we still doing that?"

"Yes, we're still doing that. Vacation people, remember?"

She grimaced at her words being thrown back at her, but she was glad to hear Penny was able to laugh about it after the prior evening. "Okay. Then let me get dressed and grab my stuff for the beach. We've got some cramming to do."

The sun was beginning to set and Penny stood blinking in the direction of the beautiful orange ball bobbing on the horizon over the ocean. She tapped a pink-polished nail against her front tooth. At any moment Paolo would lead her onto the makeshift stage that had appeared poolside at some point during the dinner hour for the Sweetheart Sweeps.

She and Lauren had spent the day sharing as many trivial facts about themselves as they could think of, still Penny could only hope she wouldn't make a total fool of herself while playing the part of Partner of Twelve Years.

She glanced over her shoulder at Lauren, who was chitchatting with the other contestants. Penny had stepped away from the group to focus on the task at hand. She ran down the list of Lauren facts in her mind. Favorite color: orange. Favorite fruit: also orange. High school mascot: tigers. If she ever needed to answer the security questions to hack any of Lauren's accounts, she was probably in good shape. The women had sat for hours, lounging in the sun and reciting their favorites, until Penny thought her head might burst from the amount of

Lauren facts she had crammed into it. When their brains were dizzy from swimming in the minutia of each other's lives, they decided on a backup plan to cover anything they might have missed. When in doubt, go with the actual facts of their short relationship. As Lauren had pointed out, they had never seen these people before, and they would never see them again.

"Hey there, Penny!"

Except for Scott. He waved one hand high in the air as he approached and carried an especially large can of beer in the other. His buddy, introduced to Penny earlier in the week as Duff, followed a few steps behind. Duff had a large can of beer in each hand. Double fisting.

"It's pounder night in the bar down by the arcade." Scott gave a sheepish grin and a shrug by way of explanation. Duff nodded along as he took a big swig of one of his drinks.

Penny smiled back, relieved at the distraction from her nerves. "What are you doing here?"

"I came to cheer you on. That's what friends do."

"Not me." Duff removed the beer can from his stubble-covered face long enough to chime in on the conversation. "I'm just here because Scott bribed me with these beers." As if to illustrate his point, he drained the last of the liquid from one can and dropped the empty container into a nearby waste bin.

"Real classy, bro." Scott shoved Duff in the shoulder before turning his attention back to Penny. "Sorry about him. We've been drinking all day."

"Yeah, I can see that." As nice as it was that Scott had come out to cheer them on, Penny didn't need the drunken distraction right before game time. Her doubt must have registered on her face, because Scott's eyes went wide as his expression shifted to someone desperate to hold onto his audience.

"Oh, wait!" He dug a sheet of folded-up paper from his back pocket and shook it out to its full size. One word, large letters inked in with scribbly lines, was written across it in blue ballpoint pen. "I even made you ladies a sign."

"LENNY?"

Scott's smile spread all the way from ear to ear. He had a big mouth and when he was happy, it seemed to take up all the real estate on his face. "I 'shipped yours and Lauren's names together, see? Lauren plus Penny equals Lenny."

In spite of herself, she laughed at the mixture of pride and kindness sparkling in Scott's eyes as he presented the sign. He was a good guy, and she appreciated having his support, but she still couldn't resist teasing him just a bit. "That's...weird. But also incredibly sweet." She reached up and gave his muscular shoulder a squeeze. "You guys should go find a good spot to watch. We're just about to get started."

"Oh, sure." He nodded dutifully, but Duff had already spun on his heel and headed toward the gathering crowd. "Good luck, Pen."

She smiled and tried to ignore the 'Pen' thing. She needed to focus, not worry about a couple of overgrown frat boys. She took a deep breath as Paolo took the stage to start the show, acting as the game show host. Accompanied by Lauren, she took her place among the panel of happy couples and prepared to compete.

"Welcome to Sweetheart Sweeps!" His voice boomed through the static-riddled speaker system. "Today our couples are playing for some fabulous prizes! Our first-place couple will receive a fifty-dollar gift card to the Waverly Winds Resort Lobby Shoppe. Second place will get a twenty-five dollar gift card. And all our couples get a ten dollar gift card to the Waverly Winds Resort Spa just for playing."

The audience clapped politely, and Penny whispered to Lauren, "Ten dollars? What are we going to do with that, get two nails polished?"

"It sure as hell isn't going to cover a massage at the Waverly Winds spa." Lauren laughed. "Maybe it would pay for a really firm handshake."

Paolo went on to explain to the crowd that the game was played much like the old *Newlywed* game from television. One member of each of the four couples would leave the stage while the other had to write their answers to Paolo's questions. When the couples were reunited, the partner who had been sequestered would attempt to match their partner's answers.

She looked from the sky to the shore to the rows of balconies trailing up the side of the resort itself—anything to keep from acknowledging the throng of people waiting to watch this competition unfold. She had to keep her nerves in check. She and Lauren had decided earlier that Penny would be the one to try to match Lauren's answers, so after Paolo introduced the couples, she headed off to the waiting area with the other contestants. As she exited the stage, she couldn't help but glance at the crowd of about fifty who had gathered in the pool area to witness the event. She took another deep breath to settle her nerves.

There was Scott, looking ridiculous but sweet, holding his Lenny sign above his head. A giggle bubbled up in her throat at the sight of her friend, relieving her of some of the tension that had built up. Duff had finished off his second pounder and moved on to a fruity drink from the poolside bar. The dude could seriously pack it away. He would regret the change in alcohol in the morning, but for the moment he looked quite pleased with himself as he chatted up a skinny blonde standing nearby.

Penny and her competition were ushered into the pool shed where they were to be sequestered until it was time to return to the stage. There was just enough room for the four of them since most of the metal racks that housed the towel supply had gone to laundry at end of the day—a fact Penny knew from her experience with the pool at the Rothmoor.

The Rothmoor. The thought of the casino hit her like a swift smack in the ass. She had been so immersed in her paradise with Lauren that her life at the Rothmoor seemed like ages ago. She had been so busy the past two days either learning everything she could about Lauren or tangled up in the sheets with her. She hadn't given her job back home a second thought. Her chest swelled and her head went dizzy with glee. Vacation people status: unlocked!

But even with that revelation, she knew she couldn't afford to linger on the thought. She had a contest to win. Being shut up in the shed was the perfect chance to size up the other competitors. Jacob, who had been married to his wife for two years, was a meathead who looked like he would be more comfortable sucking down pounders with Duff and the boys than participating in Sweetheart Sweeps. Gary was at the Waverly Winds with his wife Melissa celebrating their twenty-year anniversary. Edna was a seventy-six-year-old newlywed at the resort with her husband Bernie, and God bless them, they were at the resort on their honeymoon. Gary and his woman seemed to pose the greatest threat. You could learn a lot about a person in twenty years. Of course, Jacob and his wife, Olivia were in their early twenties and had those young, fresh brains to work with, so they couldn't be totally dismissed. As far as she could tell, it was anyone's game.

Before she could drive herself completely mad overanalyzing the situation, a staffer directed them all back to the stage. The first several questions went by in a breeze for Penny, but Jacob and Gary seemed to be struggling. Jacob and his wife laughed the whole thing off, but with each missed answer by Gary, his wife Melissa seemed to get more incensed. Penny didn't blame her. Twenty years of marriage, and the guy had only managed to get one out of seven questions right. It would have been downright sad if Penny didn't have her mind set on victory. She and Lauren were tied with the septuagenarian newlyweds, and with only three questions left to go, Penny was feeling like their chances were pretty damn good. Her heart pounded in her chest. They were pulling off their ruse.

The next question was, "Where was your first date?" Penny got that one—Game of Flats. Edna and Bernie got that point too with the answer, "the early bird special at Sizzler." The next one was favorite cocktail and Penny got that one as well, remembering Lauren's penchant for pinot grigio. Edna knew Bernie's drink was Jack on the rocks, and Jacob knew Olivia's was a margarita. Poor Gary had the misfortune of uttering the words *wine cooler*, with a half-hearted shrug, which prompted

Melissa to stand up and stomp on his foot. While he howled in pain she shrieked, "Do you know any damn thing about me, Gary Littleton?" and ran off toward the main building of the resort.

The audience cackled and hooted at this turn of events, and Penny noticed Scott was holding up his sign again. Duff had a scowl on his face and yet another beer in his hand.

"Settle down, everyone. Settle down," Paolo counseled the crowd. "We have one question left, and we're down to a tie between two couples, the Sandersons and the Hansens."

Penny tried to focus on the game and not imagine herself as Mrs. Hansen. One more question and they would win. She didn't give a damn about the gift card. It was a matter of pride. She swallowed hard and gave Lauren a wink to let her know she was confident and ready.

Paolo's voice boomed through the speakers again full of drama and bravado. "Our last question for the win is, where is your partner's favorite vacation spot?"

Lauren's favorite vacation spot? This wasn't on the laundry list of favorites that Penny had attempted to memorize about Lauren. It wasn't even a topic that had come up while they were preparing for the contest. They *did* say if they had no better answer they would use their experience together as a baseline. Should she just name Waverly Winds as the answer? It was so damn cheesy, and Penny cringed inwardly, knowing it wasn't true. She glanced at Lauren beside her. Lauren looked cool and calm as if absolutely confident that Penny should know her answer. The seconds ticked away as Penny studied Lauren's face, her own mouth partially open as if she were about to answer. She was running out of time.

"Miss Penny," Paolo prompted. "I need your answer now."

"Lauren's favorite vacation spot." Penny's words were slow and deliberate, stalling for time. Lauren's expression indicated Penny knew this one. It was the confident, serene smile and the way her chin tipped boldly upward. Penny's gaze followed Lauren's jawline to her earlobe, and that's when it caught her eye—the little pearl and emerald earring that was left over from the pair Lauren's dad had given her after the family vacation to…"Cape Cod!"

Lauren immediately flipped her answer card over to reveal her answer and held it up for the crowd to see.

CAPE COD

The audience hooted and cheered and Penny grabbed Lauren in a hug. From the crowd she heard a deep voice yell, "Way to go, Lenny!" When she looked out to wave a thank-you to Scott, she saw Duff pulling him by the arm, trying to get him to leave.

"That's correct!" Paolo confirmed. "The Hansens now lead the Sandersons nine to eight, but the Sandersons have one last chance to tie it up. Your answer please, Mrs. Sanderson."

Edna didn't hesitate. "It's Napa Valley. Bernie loves to go there. It's where his daughter and grandchildren live."

Bernie flipped his card to confirm the answer, and the crowd went wild again.

Penny leaned in close to Lauren so she could be heard over the applause. "We should really just concede to them. Edna and Bernie are adorable together. They're on their honeymoon and this will be a fun story to tell the grandkids. They're the legit winners here."

"Agreed." Lauren nodded. "We've had our fun. Let's bow out gracefully."

Their discussion was interrupted by Paolo and his microphone. "Friends, we have a tie! That means we'll play on through a tie breaker."

The audience had settled down, ready to hear what came next, and Penny raised a hand in the air in an attempt to get Paolo's attention. She wanted to concede to the older couple before things went any further.

"Just end it for fuck's sake! Those chicks aren't even a couple. They're a fraud!"

As the entire pool area went silent, Penny's line of vision went straight to Duff who was standing unsteadily on a chair. His hands were still cupped around his mouth to amplify his voice as he went on. "They're cheaters. They lied to you all."

Duff emitted a crazed, drunken howl of a laugh while Scott attempted to pull him back down to the ground.

There were gasps and shocked murmurs through the audience, and even Paolo grabbed at the chest of his white linen shirt as if he was clutching at pearls.

"What the hell?" Sweet old Edna leaned forward and growled down the row at Penny and Lauren. "What is wrong with you people?"

"So much for stepping away with class," Penny said out of the side of her mouth so only Lauren would hear. The buzz of the crowd was growing. Duff had a small group around him chanting *cheaters* over and over. "What do we do now?"

"Is this true, ladies?" Paolo demanded. His hands were balled into fists on his hips and his expression was stern and possibly a little hurt.

Lauren stood abruptly. She ignored Paolo's question and instead she turned to Penny. "We run." Lauren took Penny by the hand before loudly addressing the angry mob in front of them. "Sorry everybody."

They ran from the stage hand in hand, fleeing the scene. As they escaped the pool area, Penny thanked her lucky stars she had decided to go casual that evening in a sundress and flip-flops. She never would have been able to keep up with Lauren if she had been wearing heels. No one pursued them, but they continued to run into the building, even taking the stairs instead of waiting on the elevator in the lobby of the resort, until they finally reached their room. Lauren didn't even let go of Penny's hand until they were safely inside, at which point they both dissolved into uncontrollable giggles.

"That was a freaking fantastic rush." Lauren slid the extra lock into place then leaned her back against the door. She gulped air as she tried to catch her breath. "I can't remember the last time I had an adventure like that."

"Don't look at me." Penny kicked off her flip-flops and sank into the desk chair. "I'm a rule follower. I don't think I've ever done anything like that before."

"I don't buy that for a second. You were far too brilliant during our escape for that to have been your first time fleeing an outraged horde of vacationers."

"Well, believe it." Penny nodded solemnly. She was still sucking air, trying to steady her heartbeat to a normal pace. Running away, holding Lauren's hand, getting away with their charade as a legit couple—it was all too much.

Penny hated to admit it, but Lauren was right. As pissed off as the audience had been, it was still a hell of a lot of fun. And what was the damage, really? They hadn't accepted any prize under false pretenses. Even if they had, they had earned it. They had only missed one of the ten questions thrown their way. That couple who had been married twenty years had missed almost every single one. A nervous buzz continued to zap through Penny's core. "Do you think anyone is going to come after us?"

Lauren shook her head and moved toward the minibar by the coffeemaker. "I think we're in the clear. Although we should probably avoid the pool for the rest of our trip. And I think our days of complimentary cocktails are probably over. Speaking of, do you want a drink?"

"No thanks."

Lauren dropped some ice in a glass and poured a tiny bottle of whiskey over it before sitting down on the sofa to undo her strappy sandals. "It was fun while it lasted, I suppose."

"We probably won't have Paolo popping up at the most inconvenient times and following us around anymore either," Penny said.

"Good for you. You've found our silver lining." Lauren let out a throaty laugh and gestured at Penny to join her on the sofa. "Come over here with me and get comfortable. I think we'll be spending a lot more time in our room from here on out."

Penny took her time meandering over to Lauren, twisting her hips as she went and making her dress twirl around her legs. She slid onto the couch and tucked herself right into the crook of Lauren's arm. She tipped her head onto Lauren's shoulder and sighed contentedly. She was perfectly fine with the idea of being sequestered in the hotel room, just the two of them, for the rest of the week.

Lauren rested her free hand on Penny's thigh, right below the hem of her dress, her fingers absentmindedly strumming her skin. "I still can't believe we actually pulled it off. If we had played the tiebreaker, I think we would have won the whole damn thing."

"Yep. I'm amazed by how much I've managed to learn about you in the past four days. Isn't it cool how there are some people you just click with?"

"I've learned a lot about you as well." She kissed the top of Penny's head and shifted in her seat to face her. "For example, I know you like to be kissed just about…here."

The moment Lauren's lips met her collarbone, Penny felt a jolt that squeezed her heat between her legs. That was without a doubt the exact spot that drove her wild. Lauren had clearly learned a thing or two, and as her lips continued to trail across the hollow of her neck, Penny's thong became soaked with her lust.

"So you've learned exactly what turns me on. Well done." She dropped her head back exposing more of her neck for Lauren's attention. "I'd say you've become quite an expert at it."

Lauren continued her trail of kisses across Penny's chest as she climbed onto her lap, straddling her. Her long skirt hitched up to the top of her thighs. She rolled her hips, grinding against Penny's heat. Grabbing onto Penny's ass, Lauren squeezed and teased, sending waves of pleasure through her core.

Penny raised her head just in time to see Lauren arch her back and run her hands through her long hair. Sexy as fuck. When Lauren started to unbutton her blouse, a jolt of excitement shot right down through Penny's pussy. "You are absolutely stunning."

"As are you." Lauren winked as her lips curled into a playful grin. "Our wild adventure tonight has me all hot and bothered. I'm going to need to take these clothes off."

Every time she thought she knew this woman, she managed to surprise her all over again. Tonight Lauren was sexy in a whole new way and her stripper moves were equal parts enchanting and alluring. Penny couldn't take her eyes away and couldn't stop wondering about what Lauren may or may not be wearing under that skirt.

Lauren whipped her blouse in the air above her head like a lasso before flinging it across the room. She shook her head making her hair dance around her shoulders. Shivers worked their way through Penny's core. Being under this gorgeous woman was nothing short of absolute pleasure.

Unable to contain her curiosity any longer, Penny ran her hands up Lauren's thighs, inching under the bunched-up fabric of her skirt. Her fingertips reached a band of lace that answered some of her questions and made her pulse race. She hooked her fingers around the lacy strings and gave a slight tug. "What is this? I'd like to see it."

Lauren answered with a smirk. "I would like to talk a little more about what turns you on."

"I think seeing this would definitely turn me on."

"Well, I have something else I'd like to try as well."

Penny's mind raced and a million butterflies took flight in her belly. She didn't know what Lauren could possibly have in store for her, but she was more than open to finding out. "Bring it on."

Lauren reached for her drink on the end table and slowly lifted it to her lips. She took a sip and pulled one of the ice cubes into her mouth. Standing up, she returned the glass to its coaster on the table before slipping her skirt over her hips and down her legs. As the gauzy fabric pooled on the floor at her feet, she put her fingertips to her mouth and extracted the ice cube.

Penny's gaze remained trained on Lauren's lips as the ice slid between them. Lauren sucked the whiskey off the ice cube and positioned herself on her knees on the floor in front of her. Penny's pussy spasmed with anticipation and lust. She wanted those sexy chilled lips on her body ASAP, but Lauren seemed to be in no such rush.

She applied the ice cube to Penny's abdomen drawing a slow, wet circle around her navel. As she trailed the ice slowly down to Penny's thigh, she pressed her lips to the wetness it left behind, lightly sucking at her skin.

Penny moaned as her eyelids fluttered, heavy with lust. She squirmed under Lauren's teasing touch. Her mind bounced between wanting to know what sensation would come next and wanting to scream for Lauren to fuck her. She swallowed hard in an effort to keep her self-control intact. The ice was sliding down her other thigh when she tangled her fingers in Lauren's thick hair.

"You are driving me mad."

"So my experiment is a success then." Lauren's warm breath puffed against the cool water left behind on Penny's skin, sending another ripple of pleasure through her.

Penny moaned again in response. She squeezed her eyes shut and willed her hips to stay still despite the tingle pulsing through her core under Lauren's touch.

"How do you feel about this?" Lauren positioned her hand above Penny's heat. The melt from the ice cube dripped directly onto her clit.

Lauren didn't wait for Penny to answer—she didn't need to. It was evident in the sweet whimpers and the way Penny sucked her lower lip between her teeth that the cold melt had the effect intended. When she placed the ice against Penny's clit, her hips bucked with pleasure.

She ran her gaze down Penny's beautiful tanned body. Her slim frame had curves in all the right places. Lauren watched the muscles in Penny's graceful, long limbs tense and flex in response to the ice circling her sensitive bud.

It was more than just an appreciation of Penny's physical attributes that caused the stirring in Lauren's core. When she looked into Penny's ocean-blue eyes, she didn't just see the beauty and confidence that first attracted her, she saw the shared secrets between them. Stories that ran the gamut from first pets to first loves. The story of how afraid Penny had been when she came out to her parents as bisexual, and the joy of discovering how supportive they were. Lauren saw the hundreds of tiny details that came together to make Penny who she was. The things that made her precious to Lauren and, in turn, fueled her desire for her.

Penny's lips puckered and her eyelids fluttered again. Her high cheekbones were exquisite even as they flushed pink with want. She fixed her gaze on Lauren, heavy-lidded with a lusty look that pleaded for more.

Fireworks erupted in Lauren's chest. The ice slipped from her hand and she pressed her mouth to Penny's heat. She dug her fingertips into Penny's firm ass. She fought to hold her against her lips despite the twitching and bucking of Penny's hips. She lapped and sucked enjoying the sensation of the cold melt mingling with Penny's juices. The squirming and grinding against her face that resulted from her efforts sent a chill down Lauren's spine and she felt dampness between her own legs. Finally Penny grabbed at her head pressing it hard against her pussy, and let out a guttural growl. Her body shook with release as she came.

Lauren rocked back on her heels and swiped the back of her hand across her face. Penny wasted no time recovering. Instead she slid off the sofa to join her on the floor. Lauren was on her back with Penny on top of her before she even had time to catch her breath.

Penny inched the fabric of Lauren's thong to the side and skillfully thrummed her swollen lips with her fingers. She kissed Lauren's mouth at the same time she finally thrust into her. The long, steady strokes took Lauren quickly to the edge.

The waves of her orgasm washed over her and Lauren cried out in release. Her heat clenched and squeezed Penny's fingers still inside her. Penny nibbled at her jawline as Lauren rode out her pleasure.

Her thighs were still shaking as she pulled Penny into her arms. She sighed and planted a tender kiss on her forehead. This thing between them that Lauren had tried so hard to convince herself was merely a vacation people fling had somehow evolved. While they were learning the intimate details of each other's lives, by opening up and sharing their stories with one another, they had grown together. The inkling of an idea began to swell in Lauren's heart and tickle at the edges of her brain. This *fling* felt a lot like something more. It felt like something *real*.

CHAPTER SIXTEEN

The women lay low all Thursday, surviving on room service that they tipped exceptionally well for as a way to apologize to the resort at large. After the original excitement of their adventure from the night before had faded, Penny found herself actually laughing about the whole episode. She couldn't wait to tell her friends about it when she got back to Vegas. If Mara was proud of her before, this tale would blow her mind.

Neither Lauren nor Penny minded the break from resort life for a day. They found plenty of ways to pass the time tucked away in their hotel room together. The day turned to night and before they knew it, it was Friday—their last full day at the Waverly Winds.

Penny stood on the balcony and sipped her room-brewed, powder-creamed coffee, soaking up a little morning sun. Good coffee from the resort café was one of the sacrifices made when they decided to stay out of the public eye as much as possible. Eventually they would brave up and leave the room, hopefully slide right through the resort unnoticed. They planned to venture out and hit the beach again before the end of their vacation slipped away.

The week had gone by in a flash. Penny couldn't believe it was Friday already. She and Lauren had just really gotten started, and now it was time to end. She couldn't think about it. She wasn't supposed to think about it. She had promised Lauren she wouldn't. She had promised her a lot of things in the one week she had known her. The idea of not having Lauren by her side and no longer having to keep those promises seemed almost unbearable. But if she let herself drown in those thoughts, she would be wasting the time they had together. She tipped the last bit of the coffee left in her mug into her mouth and swallowed it down, confirming her resolve to make the most of the time she had left with Lauren. She could mourn the loss of what she and Lauren had when she was back in Vegas. Alone.

Fortunately, before she could drown in her deep thoughts, Lauren knocked on the balcony door, pulling her back to the moment. "Someone is here to see you." Her voice was muffled by the thick glass of the sliding door.

Behind Lauren, standing in the middle of the hotel room with a bouquet of tropical flowers, a bottle of wine, and a sheepish grin, was Scott Dooney. No Lenny sign or drunken Duff this time. Just him.

Lauren sauntered off to the bedroom, giving Scott a pat on the shoulder and a kind smile as she passed him. Penny gestured for Scott to sit down.

"I can't stay long. I'm actually on my way out. I just wanted to stop by before I left. I owe you an apology." He passed the bouquet to her as he spoke, then turned and set the wine on the desk.

"Oh, Scott, that wasn't your fault. Duff was right. We shouldn't have lied to everyone."

Scott hooked his thumbs in the front pockets of his jeans and hung his head in remorse. "I knew Duff was smashed, and I knew he was an ass. I should have yanked him out of the crowd well before he went off. Some guys just don't know when they've gone too far, you know?" He finally met her gaze again.

"I think his ability to draw that line may have been compromised by extreme pounder consumption." Penny frowned. Duff's behavior was a case of you reap what you sow, but Scott wasn't to blame for Duff's poor life choices. "It doesn't matter. Sure, we were embarrassed and can't show our faces at the pool for the rest of our trip. And I guess I can forget about being Facebook friends with Paolo after this. But Lauren and I had a great time the other night, and we've had a wonderful vacation together. Big picture: all's well that ends well."

Scott's expression melted to a smile of relief and he nodded as Penny summed up her week. "Team Lenny was amazing that night. It's hard to believe the two of you just met and yet you know each other so well. I guess that just goes to show when it's meant to be, it's meant to be."

Her heart wrenched. She and Lauren should have been meant to be, and yet they weren't. In twenty-four hours they were getting on two separate planes and returning to two separate homes. She had agreed with Lauren that a relationship wasn't in the stars for them. They had to go back to their separate lives. It wasn't fair, and it wasn't what Penny wanted, but *that* was what was meant to be. She blinked to ward off the tears that were building. Scott didn't need to see her cry about it. Instead she nodded her head and smiled and tried to change the subject. "So, what are you up to today? Going to the beach?"

"Actually, I'm...going home." Scott shrugged. "I've had enough of the bachelor party. Last night was another drunken repeat of the night before that and the night before that. I can't keep it up. I'm too old for it."

"Too old? Are you even thirty?"

"I'm thirty-three, thank you very much."

"But what about your brother?"

"He'll be fine. He's got his whole crew here. Honestly, I don't even think they'll notice I'm gone. A couple of the guys probably won't even sober up until a few days after they get back."

They both laughed and Penny felt another tug at her heart as she realized this was goodbye. "Well, I'll miss you. What are you going to do next?"

Scott raised his hand to the back of his head and rubbed at his hair. "Your guess is as good as mine. I'll go home after the wedding and get a job as a bouncer somewhere while I figure out where my career is going." In the black T-shirt that stretched across his muscular chest and his tight-fitting blue jeans, he already looked the part.

"I have a feeling you'll land on your feet." Penny pulled him into a hug.

"I always do," he murmured in her ear. "Goodbye, Penny."

"You have my number. Keep in touch." She gave him one last squeeze before releasing him.

Scott rubbed at his hair again as he headed toward the door. He paused briefly and gave her one last wave before walking out.

As the door closed behind him, Penny hoped she would hear from him again. She had made it through that goodbye so maybe it would serve as practice for the next, bigger, dreadful, most horrible one that was coming her way. With a sigh she went to the end table where she had set the bouquet and took a sniff of the flowers Scott had brought. Thoughtful and sweet.

"Should I be jealous?" Lauren breezed back into the room and wrapped herself around Penny. "Those are very pretty."

A tickle bubbled in Penny's middle as Lauren snaked her arms to the front of her hips. The pressure of Lauren's chest against her back was comforting. The idea of Lauren being jealous of Penny giving someone else attention was somehow comforting as well. It caused a warmth in her heart that crept up her neck and into her cheeks until she felt a prickle of threatening tears again. She took a deep breath to steady her emotions and then released it in a sigh. "It's just that saying goodbye to Scott is a reminder that our week together is almost over."

"We still have the whole day." Lauren's breath played against Penny's ear and the tender skin of her neck right beneath it. "Let's not—" She was interrupted by the chirp of her phone's text tone from the other side of the room.

"I know." Penny scrubbed her hands on her face. "I'm sorry. I know we're not doing that."

"I don't want it to end either," Lauren confessed. "But we both know the timing's just not right." Her statement was punctuated by another beep from her phone.

Penny was familiar with the *timing's not right* argument. She recalled that they had come to that conclusion. She had agreed when they determined it was best, but now she wanted to take it all back. The phone across the room beeped again, reminding her that decision was in the past and this was now. "Maybe you should get that."

"But then I'll have to stop doing this." Lauren swayed from side to side, still holding Penny against her while she trailed hungry kisses across Penny's neck.

A moan escaped Penny's lips and her head tipped back, opening herself up to more exploration. She wanted nothing more than to lose herself in the moment, forget that it was their last day together for who-knew-how-long. Maybe forever. She closed her eyes and thought back to the day before. They had spent almost all of it in bed, tangled up in each other. Neither of them had even put on real clothes from sunrise to sundown. They had spent the full twenty-four hours making love, and now Penny was left with the results. She had fallen for Lauren in spite of their conclusions and agreements. She didn't want any of it to end.

The spell was broken as Lauren's phone beeped for a fourth time.

"Ignore that," Lauren instructed as she spun Penny around so they were face-to-face. She pressed her lips firmly to Penny's. The world around them went fuzzy once more.

When the phone rang only seconds later, Penny pulled back and broke off the kiss. "Someone *really* wants to get a hold of you. You better grab that."

"Fine. But don't go anywhere. Hold that thought."

Penny put her fingertips to her lips, missing the kiss already while Lauren clicked on the call.

"Hey, what's going on?" Her brow was furrowed with concern and her free hand was balled into a fist on her hip. It was not a happy call.

Who could possibly put that expression on Lauren's face? Carolyn couldn't call her, not from her number anyway. Lauren had blocked it that first day when they were sitting by the pool. Could she have called from some other number, though? Was Carolyn on the phone right now begging Lauren to take her back? Carolyn would have the advantage once Lauren returned to Chicago. Penny would be out of sight, out of mind.

In less than twenty-four hours Lauren would be headed right back to her old life, one that could include Carolyn, and Penny would be back in Las Vegas with not even work to distract her. She still had at least a week to kill before she was welcomed back to her job at the Rothmoor. She had kept her word to Lauren and pushed all thoughts of work from her mind while they vacationed. But now that their time at the Waverly Winds was coming to an end, these unpleasant impulses were tugging at the corners of her brain. She would have to find some way to fill the empty days until she was allowed to return to the Rothmoor. And worse than that, she would have to find some way to do it while getting over Lauren.

CHAPTER SEVENTEEN

Lauren disconnected the call and slowly set the phone back down on the desk. Aware that her mouth was hanging open in shock, she quickly snapped it shut. Maybe that would help her hold in the scream of frustration she was dying to let loose. She should have expected the call, and yet somehow she found herself totally dumbstruck having actually heard the words out loud.

"Everything okay?" Penny's worried voice prompted Lauren to finally move from the spot where she had stood frozen since she hung up the phone.

Lauren slowly shook her head, still trying to process the news herself. "No. I guess not."

Penny took her hand and led her to the couch. "What happened?"

"It was James. The crew doing the work at the Hagan found more damage while they were doing the original repair. Now they're dealing with a collapsed pipe. They had James remove all of our stuff as a precaution, and the long and short of it is, the show has to be postponed." She took a deep breath. There was no sense in working herself into a panic. That wouldn't help anything.

"Postponed? For how long?"

"At least two weeks. Possibly a month. At this point they're not sure." Lauren rubbed the heel of her palms at her forehead. "I can't believe this."

Penny peeled Lauren's hand from her head and brought it to her side. She wove their fingers together as she spoke. "Can you just hold the show somewhere else? Change the venue?"

"No. James has run through all scenarios and it doesn't make sense. I'm by no means a starving artist, I have enough money to live comfortably, but I've made a financial investment in having the show at the Hagan. I don't have so much money that I have the ability to throw it around all devil-may-care, especially now that I'm the only income for my household." She pressed her lips together tightly. Those were the facts, and this was what had to be done. "No, there's nothing I can do until they let us back in. I just have to wait it out, and it will be fine."

"You sound like me." Penny tipped her head onto Lauren's shoulder with a heavy sigh. "We're both going back home to sit around and wait on our jobs. Aren't we a pair."

"No kidding."

The truth was, putting together the show at the Hagan had been a wonderful distraction from her breakup with Carolyn. Lauren didn't want her back and she didn't miss *her*. There was just something disheartening about sitting around an empty house all alone with no job to go to and no project to complete. *And that was exactly how Penny must have felt all this time.*

It was no wonder that Penny had seemed so glum about the vacation drawing to a close. "You can expect a lot of texts from me in the next couple of weeks. We'll keep each other company until we get back to our normal lives. Maybe we'll play some Words with Friends."

"Wait." Penny shifted in her seat and faced Lauren. Her eyebrows shot up and excitement lit up her face like a kid learning school has been canceled for a snow day. "There's nothing you can do but sit around and wait. You said it yourself. And I'm heading back to Vegas to do the exact same thing. Why are we going to be alone playing games online when we could be playing Scrabble together?"

"Is that some kind of innuendo?"

"I'm serious. Stay with me in Vegas for a while."

Stay. With Penny. In Vegas. For a while. No, she couldn't possibly do it. Not that she didn't want to. Another week of falling asleep tangled up with Penny. Another week of waking up next to her. It sounded like heaven. It was more than the physical. In the past few days she had watched Penny shed her tough, all-business exterior and really let go, all because Lauren had dragged her along on this wild adventure. Penny was beautiful, vivacious, smart and funny, and while they were biding their time in this tropical paradise, Lauren had fallen head over heels for her.

She was doing her damnedest to keep the feeling under wraps. They had agreed that neither of them was ready to jump into a relationship and that they both needed to return home and get a handle on their lives. That was what made sense. Lauren had to stick to that and not let her heart overrule her head, no matter how brightly those blue eyes shone at her with excitement at the idea.

"I can't." Lauren shook her head. It was the responsible answer to give. "I have to go home to Chicago."

"No, you don't." Penny stuck her chin out defiantly and challenged her. "You totally just said it. There's nothing you can do but sit and wait. You don't have to be in Chicago to do that. You can sit and wait just fine in Las Vegas. Best of all, you can sit and wait with me. I have some sitting and waiting of my own to do, you know."

"I know, but…" But what? It was absolutely true that Lauren would be going home to an empty house and no job to do. Sure, she could start searching for inspiration for her next project, but that was yet another thing she could do, as Penny put it, *just fine in Vegas.*

Would another week with Penny only make it even harder to leave her? Probably. Lauren could tell herself that she could be reasonable and walk away when their time was up, but with each passing day her heart had ached a little more at the prospect.

"But?" Penny prompted. She had both of Lauren's hands in hers and a thrilling buzz of possibility passed between them. Her eyes were wide and hopeful and impossibly beautiful.

How could Lauren possibly deny herself some more time with Penny? Besides, if she went back to Chicago she would have to face all the crap she still needed to sort through that Carolyn had abandoned when she moved out. And she would probably hound James asking for updates on the Hagan until he went completely mad. When she framed it that way, the choice was undeniably clear.

"Okay. I'll do it."

CHAPTER EIGHTEEN

Lauren flipped her large-framed sunglasses down from where they had been resting on her head to cover her eyes. Somehow the sunshine in Las Vegas seemed even brighter than it had been at the Waverly Winds. The sun in both locations was undoubtedly brighter than Lauren was used to in Chicago. She shook her hair behind her as she walked down the sidewalk hand in hand with Penny. "It's Vegas, baby!"

Penny laughed and tightened her grip. "You've been here before. In fact, you were just here a week ago." She swung their hands between them. Carefree. Happy. Lovers.

"Hey, I'm just taking it all in." Lauren grinned. "Extended vacation people!"

Penny stopped in her tracks, effectively tugging Lauren to a halt as well. "It's officially time to drop that."

"Okay, okay. It's dropped," Lauren agreed with a sheepish shrug.

The women laughed and continued on their way to the café.

After their Saturday afternoon flight they had gone directly back to Penny's suite at the Rothmoor. Tired and uncomfortable from a morning of traveling, they showered then promptly collapsed on the large, white L-shaped sofa in Penny's living room. They didn't leave the suite for the rest of the day. When they needed anything, Penny rang up room service and they continued their day of lounging around.

But Sunday morning was a different story. Penny and her circle of friends had a standing brunch date at Café Gato, their favorite hangout as Lauren recalled from memorizing Penny's list of favorites. So, after a solid night of sleep on Penny's very comfortable and plush bed, they rose with the sun and got dressed to meet the gang for brunch.

Café Gato was just as Penny had described it when they were on the beach. From the colorful, mismatched coffee cups to the large, orange tabby sunbathing in the window seat at the front of the shop, the place oozed cozy charm and hip hangout style. The women grabbed a cup of coffee from the bar as soon as they entered. The rich, warm aroma of freshly brewed coffee enveloped them as Penny led Lauren to a table right in the center of the shop.

As Penny introduced her to the women she hadn't met the last time she was in town and they all said their hellos Lauren felt the joyful sense of belonging. She had heard so much about these women from Penny. She felt as if she had known them all for years as well. Mara, Penny's best friend and a comedian at the Rothmoor, had been holding court when they arrived, telling a story that had all the others laughing. Frankie had a cat in her lap, which fit with everything Lauren had heard about her being an animal lover. Frankie even worked at the animal shelter next door to the café. Then there were Jenna and Hayleigh, artist and dancer, and together the couple who couldn't keep their hands off each other. They were as cute as could be.

Penny and Lauren settled into their seats while the group wasted no time, bombarding Penny with questions about the trip.

"How was the vacation?"

"Why don't you have more of a tan?"

"Did you really get stuff comped the whole time you were there?"

"When are you going back to work?"

Penny smiled as she shook her head and waved her hands in front of her as if to direct their questions like traffic. "It was a wonderful vacation and I have returned much more relaxed than I left. Also, the Waverly Winds Resort may very well be the cheesiest place on Earth. I highly recommend it."

"Wow." Hayleigh's big blue eyes went rounder. "'Cheesiest place on Earth' is quite a statement from a born and bred Vegas girl."

Lauren nodded along with the conversation, but kept quiet, giving Penny the chance to reconnect with her friends.

"Isn't that the truth," Penny continued. "As for work, I won't be returning for at least a week. I have to meet with my father to get that cleared."

"It won't be a minute too soon," Mara quipped. "Everybody misses you. I think Timothy has driven half the staff barking mad."

"Timothy?" Penny repeated the name questioningly as if waiting for Mara to expand on the throwaway comment. Lauren recognized that name from the stories Penny shared on the beach as well. "What's Timothy managed to get himself up to while I've been...away?"

"Well, for one, your dad has him filling in on your shifts." Mara wiggled her eyebrows indicating this was interesting news. "Literally walking the casino floor. Needless to say, he's been a real bitch."

Penny raised her own eyebrows at that revelation. "I can imagine. And what's been going on with security?"

Mara shrugged. "I don't know if anything's been decided behind the scenes. We've had those same guys from the temporary contractor."

Lauren sipped her coffee and tried her best to read the expression on Penny's face. Penny's lips were pressed tightly closed like she was trying to hold in her next thought.

As quickly as it had come on, the tension on Penny's face melted away, and she deftly changed the subject. "Enough about the casino. What else did I miss?"

"Frankie broke up with Maisy," Hayleigh offered, but when Jenna elbowed her in the ribs she gave the group a sheepish grin as if regretting her hasty gossip. "I mean, Penny asked."

"No, it's fine. It's true." Frankie reached over and patted Hayleigh's forearm in a forgiving gesture. "I did break up with Maisy."

Penny looked genuinely surprised. "That was fast."

"Yep," Jenna agreed in her smug, tell-it-like-it is manner. "It's like Frankie is the new Mara."

The comment was met with groans and hoots from all around the table. Lauren caught the meaning of that one too. Penny had told her all about how Mara had a reputation as an incurable playgirl.

"You and Maisy were too much alike. It just couldn't work." Hayleigh sighed and shook her head empathetically. "That's why they always say opposites attract. It's just science."

Lauren couldn't help but smile at the words of wisdom coming from the youngest member of the group. Hayleigh's viewpoint seemed to be evidenced by her relationship with Jenna. The women couldn't have been more opposite in appearance. Jenna with her short, dark hair combed into a faux-hawk, and her flannel and denim style versus Hayleigh's blond hair, blue-eyed, all-American girl next door look. But there must have been a common thread that bound them together so tightly. It was apparent in the way they stole adoring glances at each other. It was appallingly sweet.

"We must be boring you to death." Frankie reached over and gave Lauren's shoulder a friendly squeeze. "Tell us more about you. I heard you're a photographer. I think that's fascinating. Penny said you have a big show coming up, is that right?"

"It is." She appreciated being included in the conversation, even if she suspected Frankie was mostly trying to push someone else into the spotlight so the heat would be off her and the Maisy breakup. "We've run into a slight speed bump as far as opening, which is why I'm able to spend this time here in Vegas, but it should be all systems go in about a week."

Jenna leaned forward and propped her chin on her fists, clearly interested in hearing more. "What's the theme of your show?"

Penny sat back in her chair and beamed with joy. Being surrounded by her friends once again felt wonderful, and the fact that Lauren had fit in with the bunch so easily was the syrupy sweet cherry on the sundae.

Currently she was answering the group's many questions about her photography and the upcoming show. Penny admired the poise and grace she possessed as she fielded the inquiries. It was so different from what Penny was used to, her last relationship having been with a strong, silent type.

Relationship. Was that what she and Lauren had? It sure wasn't the pretend couple thing they had been doing at first, but there was still an end date in sight for them. That wasn't an element of a typical relationship, at least not any Penny had ever been a part of. Sitting in the café with Lauren and her friends felt...normal. It was a feeling she wanted to hold on to even harder with each passing day.

She blinked to get rid of the thought of Lauren's actual departure and took a sip of her coffee. Mara was quizzing Lauren on the particulars of the Sweetheart Sweeps story from their vacation. Lauren's face lit up with pride as she recounted their near victory.

At least the conversation had steered far away from life at the Rothmoor, but Penny was still inwardly cringing at the mention of Timothy earlier. She did enjoy hearing that the man who had been so pleased to send her packing ended up having to cover her shifts on the casino floor. That was like a demotion for him. Timothy tried his damnedest to keep up a rivalry between the two of them, but Penny had never much felt an enthusiasm for it. She was the daughter of the Rothmoor casino dynasty; he was her father's minion. One day she was going to own the casino whether she worked there or not, but she wanted to be worthy of it. That was exactly the reason why she needed to come up with an idea to fix the mess Bryce had made with the security crew at the Rothmoor and present it to her father ASAP. It would show him she was back on top of her professional game.

The solution was there in front of her somewhere. She could sense it pinging at the edge of her psyche, a weird just-out-of-reach feeling. At any moment it could fade away without her having the chance to wrap her arms around the answer, or she could grab it by the horns and wonder what the hell had been so hard about finding it in the first place. It was there; she was certain. She just needed to identify it, develop it, and present it to her father.

She exhaled and did her best to arrange her features into an expression that indicated she was following her friends' conversation, even though her mind was wandering. God, she missed work. And now that they had returned to Las Vegas and she and Lauren agreed they were leaving the vacation people pact behind them, Penny really had the best of both worlds— sexy woman to spend her days and nights with and the freedom to obsess about her career to her heart's content.

The waiter delivering a tray of pastries to their table and refilling coffee mugs was enough of a distraction to snap Penny back to the conversation at the table.

Mara summed it up after a few disappointed clicks of her tongue. "So you made a friend who ended up selling you out for alcohol and chuckles. How rude."

"No," Lauren corrected. "It was the friend's friend who got shit-faced and drummed up an angry mob who practically torched and pitchforked us into seclusion for the remainder of the trip."

"Not that we minded much." Penny raised a suggestive eyebrow and grinned at her friends. "Besides, I think that version of the story may have been a little dramatic. Actually, Scott was a really great guy. He came to our room and apologized for everything. He even ended up leaving the Waverly Winds before his vacation was up because he was tired of the juvenile behavior of the other guys he was there with. He had a lot on his mind anyway since he had basically just lost his job and he needed to figure out what he was going to do next... Oh, my god."

How could she have not seen it before? The solution to the security staff situation at the Rothmoor really might have been right in front of her that whole time. She just needed to put two and two together.

"Hey, are you okay?" Lauren's brow furrowed with concern, clearly noticing the sudden shift in Penny's tone.

"I am." Penny gave Lauren's hand a reassuring squeeze before pushing back her chair and standing. Her heart was pounding with determination and her head was light and tingling with excitement. Inspiration had struck. "Excuse me for just a minute. I need to make a quick call."

Later that evening after Penny set her business plan in motion and had an elegant dinner with Lauren at the Daisy Jane, they returned to the suite and made love once again. When they were both finally spent, she rolled onto her side and nuzzled into the crook of Lauren's arm just above her breast. "Hey, I have a surprise for you."

Lauren twisted to look her in the eye and smiled mischievously. "More surprising than when you took your tongue and—"

"I'm serious." Penny giggled despite her words. Heat crept into her cheeks remembering the moment mentioned. "I don't want you to leave."

"I'm tucked in for the whole night." She pulled the sheet up over her hip. "I'm not going anywhere. I promise."

Penny placed her palm on Lauren's taut abs, holding her in place. "No. I don't want you to leave Las Vegas. And I have a plan. An offer."

"Oh babe, I love it here with you, and this time together has been absolutely incredible, but I can't stay. My work is in Chicago."

"That's what I'm talking about. What if your work was here?"

Lauren wriggled out from under her and propped herself up on her elbows, positioning herself to have a more face-to-face discussion. "My work...here? Penny, I've got a show opening in Chicago in, well, soon. But it's definitely in Chicago where people know me. Where I have a reputation."

"I mean *after* that show." Penny shifted on the mattress and sat up. The conversation was not going the way she had planned it in her mind. She was explaining it all wrong. Lauren was supposed to be excited too, or at least more open to the idea of staying. "After the show at the Hagan is complete, you could move here with me. Or maybe not *here* with me, if that's too soon, but here in Las Vegas. You can move your work here."

Lauren still didn't look as enthused as Penny felt about the plan. "Penny, it's not that simple. I would need a place to work. I would have to find all new venues for shows. There's a lot more to what I do than just taking pictures. I've made a name for myself in Chicago. Here I would be back at square one."

"No, I've thought that through," Penny argued. "Everything is virtual these days. You wouldn't necessarily lose your Chicago patrons. That's the beauty of the Internet! Besides, I've already got a foot in the door for you. You can open a show here, at the Rothmoor. There's a great space on the second floor of the casino near the ballroom and the Laffmoor that's been vacant for over six months. I'll just ask my father if you can use it. I'll show him your website. I know he'll love your work."

Hurt flashed in Lauren's green eyes as if she had been slapped across the face. Struck. "So your father is going to float me?" She shook her head vehemently. "Absolutely not. Anyway, a space in a casino is not what I need to get my work shown. There's just not enough of the right kind of traffic."

How could the conversation be going so wrong? Presenting projects to the board of the casino had never given her as much trouble as she was having explaining the whole thing to Lauren. This was supposed to be good news. "It's not like that at all," Penny argued.

"That's *exactly* how it sounds to me." Lauren scrubbed her hands over her face. "Look, Penny, it's taken me a damn long time to earn my reputation as a photographer. A shit ton of pushing through rejection, soldiering on through late nights, struggling through the lean times, and generally working damn hard at what I do. But that's the thing. I've *earned* it. It's part of what makes my story what it is. I'm proud of how far I've come and what I've accomplished. I've worked my whole life for what I've got. No one has ever just handed me opportunities on a silver platter."

It was Penny's turn to recoil. "Just because my family owns the casino doesn't mean I haven't earned my place in it. I've worked here since I was fourteen years old. I went to college, earned a degree in business, came back here in an entry-level position and worked my way up to management. I'm not just Daddy's little princess who gets to do whatever she pleases." The sting of tears at the back of her eyes could have been due to sadness from Lauren not agreeing to stay in Vegas, or from anger that she had to defend herself and her job at the Rothmoor. Her emotions were like a train going off the rails, nothing but destruction and heartbreak ahead and nothing she could do to stop it.

Fortunately, Lauren's expression softened once again as she grabbed Penny and wrapped her in her arms, lightly kissing the top of her head. "I'm sorry. I didn't mean to imply that about you at all. I know how important you are to the casino, I can tell by the way your friends talk about you. I believe one hundred percent that you deserve everything you have here." She took a deep breath before continuing. "All I was saying was this is *my* story. I just wanted you to understand where I'm coming from. And why I can't just accept a handout from your father."

Penny sniffed and a tear slid down her cheek. "It wouldn't be a *handout*. It's like I said, a foot in the door. Your photos would be—"

"Shh." Lauren cut her off. She rubbed her palm down Penny's bare arm. Soothing her. "I can't accept it. I have to go back to Chicago. To my art. We knew this was how it was going to be. We knew we were going to have to go back to our separate lives eventually."

"I know." Penny choked back a sob. "I just didn't know it was going to be so hard."

"Let's not think about it yet. We have at least a week together. Possibly more. Let's agree to enjoy what we have while we have it."

Penny swallowed hard and nodded. She was lucky to have this extra time with Lauren. She snaked her arms around her again and kissed her hard on the mouth. She needed to be as close to Lauren as possible and to work off the adrenaline from their spat. Another round of orgasms seemed like the perfect way to do both of those things and seal their agreement as well.

CHAPTER NINETEEN

Two days after their brunch at Café Gato, Lauren laid back on Penny's couch and waited for her to come out of her room dressed and ready in her professional best for her meeting with the Rothmoor's board of directors.

The women had spent the day before developing Penny's plan, first getting all the details organized, then preparing Penny's presentation. Finally Lauren played devil's advocate in a mock Q&A, anticipating how Timothy would try to put the brakes on the project and maintain his upper hand in the company by any means possible. The whole experience had been very reminiscent of the cram sessions on the beach preparing for the Sweetheart Sweeps. Only this time Penny was the real deal and she was ready to get the job done.

Lauren's heart swelled with admiration at Penny's passion for the project. Even though Lauren had been adamant about her relaxing while they were away on vacation, she really respected Penny's ambition and dedication to her career. Watching her in action the past couple days had been amazing. A whole new side of Penny had been revealed, a side that endeared Penny to her even more.

"Are you almost ready? You don't want to be late," Lauren called out.

"I'm never *late*."

Lauren smiled. Penny was a prompt perfectionist, and she certainly did not need anyone hounding her about getting out the door on time. Lauren had an ulterior motive for pushing her. She was anxious to see the finished product. As much as she despised the politics of business, the thought of Penny wearing a suit with her hair swept up into a sexy bun and in command of a boardroom made the concept much more appealing.

She supposed it was a hazard of being an artist that she was prone to following her heart over her head. She had really gone and done it this time. She was falling more and more for Penny with each passing day. She was enjoying her extended stay with Penny and her time in Vegas. She even managed to slide right into Penny's friend circle, which was no small feat in the lesbian world.

Lauren didn't have a friend circle like that back in Chicago. She had been so wrapped up in her art and her life with Carolyn for so long that she hadn't actually taken the time to cultivate and maintain many friendships. Any friends she had tended to fade into the background. That was exactly what had happened with Shelly Rothmoor. Shelly got wrapped up in Gerald Rothmoor, Lauren had gone on with her life back home and while love bloomed for her bestie, their friendship wilted.

Sure, she had James in her life, but he was her employee and that put lines in place that weren't to be crossed. They enjoyed working together and they could talk about photography for hours, but outside of work they weren't really friends.

"The bitch is back, baby!" Penny announced grandly as she entered the living room.

Lauren stopped her internal pity party and turned her attention to the vision of beauty approaching her. Penny was absolutely stunning in a gray suit and black Louboutins with a three-inch heel. The silver threads in the fabric of her jacket caught the light as she moved, and the resulting shimmer drew and held the eye. She was like a shark ready to attack, a really damn sexy shark. "You look fierce and ready to do battle. Seriously, you look fantastic."

"I *feel* fantastic." Penny smiled radiantly and confidence shone in her eyes. "I am *so* excited to get back to work. Once my father hears this plan, all will be forgiven and I can get back to it."

"Not until I take you to dinner tonight to celebrate."

"And don't forget about drinks tonight with the girls at Flats," Penny added.

Their schedule was set. Lauren was going to enjoy a little nickel slot play in the casino while Penny set the business world on fire. Then they would meet back at the suite to regroup and get ready for a romantic dinner out. Finally, they would wrap up the night with drinks and dancing with Penny's friends at the lesbian bar.

"Ah, Game of Flats," Lauren said as she took Penny by the hand and twirled her around. "Back to where it all began."

Penny slid behind her and rested her chin on Lauren's shoulder. "Think you can handle it?" Her warm breath caused a shiver down Lauren's spine. The lesbian bar she could handle, although this in charge, no-nonsense, all business, sexy as fuck Penny might give her a run for her money.

"I'll do more than handle it," she purred back. "I have plans for you that will make you forget there was anything at all before this night."

"I'm going to hold you to that." Penny smirked before planting a kiss on Lauren's cheek. "But first, I'm off to save the world."

"At least you're not dramatic about it."

"Hold on." Penny held up a hand halting the conversation. "I need my lucky chip." She dashed back into her room. When she emerged again, she was holding a casino chip from the Rothmoor victoriously in the air. "Now I'm set."

"You carry a lucky chip?"

"That's just what I call it. It's more like a reminder of something."

"A reminder that your family owns a casino?"

Penny stuck her tongue out at her in response and defiantly stuck the plastic disc under the lace of her bra where it couldn't be seen. "No, smartass. It's a five-dollar chip that reminds me that I make my own luck. Anytime someone has a chip just like this one in the casino they have a choice. They can hold on to what they have or they can take a chance. This chip reminds me to go after what I want."

"I get that." Lauren nodded. "I'm proud of you going after what you want today. I have a very good feeling about it."

"That's what I'm talking about, baby." Penny gave her a wink.

As Penny flitted about the room gathering her phone, keys, and anything else she needed for the day, Lauren filled a Rothmoor Towers travel coffee mug for her to take along. Like a dutiful wife she handed it to her as they kissed goodbye. "Go get 'em, gorgeous."

"Thanks, babe." Penny hoisted her buttery leather bag up on her shoulder. "I'll see you this afternoon. Enjoy your day in the casino."

Lauren stood frozen in the doorway after Penny left. The exchange of terms of endearment now came as naturally as it would if they were an actual couple. *Except we're not* a little voice reminded her.

Seeing Penny restored back to her business-suited self blew Lauren away. It was clear Penny had her spark back, and it was also clear Penny's job really was everything to her. Lauren couldn't imagine Penny ever wanting to leave the casino behind. Lauren blew out a breath and shook her head to bring herself back to reality. This was Penny's world where she belonged. Just like Lauren belonged in Chicago. She had to remember that. What happened in Vegas would stay in Vegas.

Penny stared at the panel of numbers above the door and tapped her pointed-toe shoe against the floor. Somehow the bravado she'd displayed in front of Lauren back in her suite had diminished rapidly as if it was keeping pace with the descending elevator car.

It wasn't just pitching her candidate for Head of Security at the Rothmoor to the board that was eating at her, it was pitching her candidate in front of her father.

She lifted her arms to let some air flow to her pits. She needed to stay cool, calm, and collected—or at least she needed to *appear* that way. Go time was no time to panic.

This was her moment to shine and she was going to make the most of it. She would march herself into that boardroom and take control the way she used to before the whole mess with Bryce went down. She could do that. She *had* to do that because it was time to show she was ready to get back to work. As the doors slid open, she threw her shoulders back and stuck her chin out as she strode toward the boardroom. She made it exactly eight steps before she stopped dead in her tracks and her stomach seized into a tangle of knots.

Her father was waiting for her outside of the room. Her heart gave a hard, unnatural thump in her chest, but she forced herself to keep moving. There was no running from him anymore. She deserved her spot in the company and she had a plan to make things right again. She swallowed hard, bit the inside of her cheek, and approached him directly.

There he stood in his crisp, sand-colored business suit, his salt-and-pepper hair neatly coiffed. He seemed to get bigger the closer she got. His hands were tucked in his pockets and he lifted the toes of his neatly polished wingtips joyfully off the floor. A smile spread across his face and his shoulders relaxed as she stepped in front of him. "Penny, dear, you have been missed around here. It's good to have you back. You've been a very hard woman to reach lately." He gave her a knowing look, but his eyes sparkled with kindness. "How are you, Henny Penny?"

There was no sign of the stern reprimand she had been expecting from him. He had even called her by his pet name. Penny let out her breath and the tension drained from her neck and upper back. Her father was clearly happy to see her and he was treating her the same way he always had. "Dad." She blinked hard against the sting of tears threatening at the back of her eyes. She couldn't get emotional before presenting to the board. "I'm sorry. I know I should have returned your call. Timothy said you *strongly recommended* I take a vacation—a break from work—so I did. Then I just continued to lie low when I got back. But I couldn't do it anymore. Lying low and doing nothing is not very me."

He chuckled, a deep warm sound, and shook his head. "No, it's not very you at all. And I would've never asked you to go against your nature like that. Timothy took things a little too far and I apologize for sending him when I should have talked to you myself. I did want you to take a vacation. You and Bryce had just broken off your engagement, your job is demanding, and you work damn hard at it. You never take a break and I was genuinely worried about you. I didn't want you to work yourself into the ground." He took her hand, not in a business handshake way, but in a gentle, loving Dad way. Just like he used to when she was a little girl and he would take her to the park to people watch while they sat on a park bench eating ice cream from the vendor cart. "You need to take some time away every now and again. You never do, but it's good for you."

She smiled back at her father, remembering how he had always made time for her, even when he was busy running the casino. As a boss he had always been tough but fair. Lately she hadn't been very fair to him. She avoided him when she should have had the guts to stand up for herself. Believing what Timothy had told her hadn't done her any favors. Her father had just wanted what was best for her. "I think I finally get that."

"Good." He squeezed her hand before he released it and gave her a stiff nod of encouragement. "Now, get into that boardroom and show everyone exactly how damn good you are at your job."

Lauren hung out in the suite until just before noon when her rumbling stomach indicated that the coffee and granola bar she ate in lieu of breakfast wasn't going to carry her any further. She grabbed a quick bite in the café on the first floor and then headed out to try her luck in the casino, but after losing two twenties in the nickel slots, she was over hanging out alone in the casino. She walked a few laps of the main floor, people watching and killing time.

The Rothmoor was the picture of golden era casino décor with its high ceilings accented with gilded and rich red tapestries lining the walls. Enormous gold and crystal chandeliers hung above the main promenade, which was lined with floor-to-ceiling columns painted red, black, and gold in an art-deco style. It was beautiful, grandiose, and fun. If the size of the crowd was any indication, it hit the mark for drawing people in.

Those people were a whole other fascinating subject. Even at one o'clock in the afternoon there were people dressed to the nines—women in slinky cocktail dresses, jewels and gems adorning their slim necklines and wrists and men in sports coats and wingtips, their upper-crust expensive haircuts and bleached smiles high on the thrill that was gambling in Las Vegas.

But not every patron had that high-class polish. There were just as many tourists clad in floral-print garb and grandmas in sweatshirts with pictures of cats on them. It was a striking contrast and yet somehow perfectly normal with the culture of this gambling mecca. The scene made Lauren itch for her camera, although she knew taking pictures in a casino was a taboo of the highest order.

So after a brief stop back in Penny's suite, Lauren found herself meandering up and down the Vegas strip, snapping photos of the life happening around her. Most of the people outside of the casino didn't seem to notice her taking pictures. Those that did—like the older couple she snapped grinning mirthfully at each other while standing next to a larger than life statue of a gladiator—didn't seem to mind.

It wasn't long before she was in the *zone*. The joy of getting lost in her art brought her to life. When she finally made her way back to the Rothmoor a little over an hour later, she was totally afloat on the rush of doing what she loved most in life. Buoying her even more was the anticipation of her celebratory dinner and night out with Penny.

"Lauren Hansen, you are one hard woman to find." Carolyn had been seated on one of the large, round cream and gold brocade settees in the lobby when Lauren pushed through the heavy glass doors. As their gazes met, Carolyn jumped into action and sauntered toward her. There was a look of seduction in her heavy-lidded gaze that Lauren hadn't seen cross her face in a couple of years. Unfortunately, at this point, it was not a welcome look. It was much more alarming than sexy.

"I'm what?" Solid thinking and the art of conversation seemed to have completely left her mind. Carolyn was the last person she expected to see in Las Vegas, and her appearance in the lobby of the Rothmoor had apparently short-circuited her brain. But anger that the woman who had so deviously broken her heart was now invading her space quickly bubbled inside her. There was a good reason she had kept her distance from Carolyn since they broke up. The very sight of her filled Lauren with disgust. "What the hell are you doing here?"

Carolyn's lips curled into a pout as she reached Lauren's side. She brushed her fingertips down the length of Lauren's arm and blinked up at her through her thick, mascara-caked lashes. "I expected a friendlier greeting than that. Didn't you miss me at all?"

Lauren managed to pull her hand away before Carolyn captured it in her own. She took a deep breath, struggling to keep her emotions in check and her voice at an acceptable volume for a conversation in public. She ignored the question and repeated her own. "What are you doing here?"

"I've been trying to reach you by phone, but my calls wouldn't go through."

Of course her calls didn't go through. Lauren had blocked Carolyn's number that day by the pool at the Waverly Winds and never changed it back in her phone settings. So those calls wouldn't have gone through. They would have just fizzled out there somewhere in the ether.

None of that mattered as Carolyn continued without waiting for an explanation. "I couldn't get James to reach out to you on my behalf either. First time I've ever seen him eager to mind his own business, to be honest. Luckily I was able to coax your mysterious whereabouts out of him."

Lauren didn't appreciate the dig on her assistant, nor did she care for the way Carolyn was attempting to insert herself back in her life. A tourist heading for the casino bumped into her shoulder as he passed, and suddenly she was very aware that the two of them were having a private conversation while standing in the middle of a lobby full of people. But she wasn't interested in inviting her ex to have coffee or grab something to eat. Her stomach twisted at the thought. She wasn't interested in spending any more time with her ex at all. Carolyn hadn't even explained her reason for needing to get in touch with her. Was there some kind of emergency? "Carolyn, what are you doing here in Las Vegas?"

"Is there somewhere we can talk?" Carolyn said gravely. She lowered her voice and her demeanor shifted to a more subtle vibe.

"Oh my god, is something wrong?" Lauren's head was spinning. There was no way in hell she was taking her ex to Penny's suite to have a conversation, but if there was some kind of dire news they needed to discuss, the middle of the lobby wasn't the appropriate place for it either.

"I miss you," Carolyn blurted out, her voice suddenly not so quiet. "I've come here to tell you I'm sorry and to beg you to give us another chance."

Another chance? Was this woman for real? Of all the things Carolyn could have marched back into her life to say, this one blew her mind. Emotions seared through Lauren's core, pulling at her heart from many directions—hurt, surprise, disgust, and mostly anger that Carolyn would even have the audacity to try a stunt like this. On top of it all, she became painfully aware that they were a source of entertainment for casino goers loitering in the lobby. Snapping out of her fog, she grabbed Carolyn firmly by the upper arm and led her out of the lobby and down a hall that, according to signage, led to maintenance and the security office.

"Are we going to your room?" Carolyn tripped over her own feet as she struggled to keep up with Lauren's pace.

"No," Lauren said curtly and definitively as they jerked to a stop. She estimated they were far enough down the hallway that they wouldn't be overheard. At least they wouldn't be a public spectacle. "No, we are not going to my room. I'm not going *anywhere* with you, and I'm sure as hell not taking you back. Not today, not ever." She needed to get a handle on her anger. Sounding like a pop princess breakup song was no way to be taken seriously.

"Laurie, listen to me," Carolyn pleaded. "I made a mistake. I shouldn't have left you. I'm sorry. I need you. I know that now."

Lauren shook her head. She would not be pulled in with an old lover's nickname. "You did make a mistake in the way you treated me. In the way you treated *us*. But I doubt you even mean that apology sincerely. And that's the whole problem here. I will *never* be able to trust you again. That's not going to change whether I forgive you or not."

Carolyn looked dumbstruck, but tiny storms were brewing in her eyes. An angry blush crept up her neck and into her cheeks. She remained silent for the moment, so Lauren went on.

"You fucked us up when you decided you wanted to sleep with someone else. Let me be perfectly clear. I am not in love with you anymore, and I never will be again."

"You need me too," Carolyn sputtered desperately. "I know you do. I'm your muse. Remember how we used to work so well together? Hell, you've got photos of me in your upcoming show. James told me."

The photographs that would be featured in the show at the Hagan had been written up for publicity materials months ago and released to the public shortly after. James had made no breach of duty by discussing them with Carolyn. The only mistake James had made was not realizing Lauren had made a change to what she was displaying in the show—and that was because Lauren hadn't told him yet. No, this was plainly an attempt by Carolyn to gaslight Lauren into thinking her loyal assistant was turning on her.

"I *had* photos of you in the show. They've been removed." Lauren's words had the impact she intended based on the way Carolyn's face went from beet red to pale as parchment. She couldn't deny there was a time that Carolyn had been a source of inspiration for her art, back when they were in love and the possibilities for their future had been endless. But Lauren's art had gone on just fine when Carolyn had left her. Inspiration was all around her. It wasn't dependent on the whim of one woman, and certainly not a woman who would betray her. "Since the opening of the show was delayed, I had time to make some changes. Silver lining, I suppose."

Carolyn's eyes narrowed to slits and ugly anger took over her face. Her story changed along with her demeanor. "I hope you're telling me the truth about those photos because I do not give you permission to use my image in your work. And if I find out you have, you *will* be hearing from my attorney. I swear to god, I will ruin you."

The change from cajoling ex-lover to desperate snake bitch would have alarmed Lauren months ago, but after Carolyn's betrayal of their relationship, it didn't surprise her one bit. She waited until the last nasty word was spat before responding.

"Have at it. But if it's not through your attorney, don't ever contact me again." Lauren turned on her heel and, without so much as a glance over her shoulder, left Carolyn behind for good.

CHAPTER TWENTY

Penny couldn't stop smiling as she said goodbye to Scott and disconnected their Skype call. Her father had been impressed with Scott's credentials when Penny had presented them, but once he had the chance to interview him via Skype, the deal was sealed. He had hired Scott on the spot to head security at the Rothmoor. Her plan had been a blazing success.

Timothy's hand shot up in the air like a teacher's pet in a classroom waiting to be called on to speak.

"Timothy, do you have something to add?" Penny's father had been ready to dismiss everyone before the gesture, and he seemed put off by the interruption.

"I wonder if we're acting a little hasty hiring this Mr. Dooney without actually meeting him in person." Timothy's face scrunched up in distaste. "You know, confirm he's actually who he *says* he is."

"I have met him in person," Penny said, ready to do battle to defend Scott if needed.

To her relief, her father waved a hand dismissively in the air. "Mr. Dooney will be subjected to the same background checks all of our high security hires are, of course. I think Penny's judgment was just as fine in Hawaii as it is here in Vegas. She has met Mr. Dooney and recommends him highly. I trust her opinion." He turned his attention to Penny. "Additionally, to that end, Penelope, I think you're more than ready to return to your position here at the Rothmoor."

Penny's heart soared at the sound of the words out loud. She was hoping to get Scott in as the new head of security at the casino, and she loved knocking Timothy down a peg or two, but until she actually heard her father say she could come back to work, she wasn't completely satisfied. Finally she could let out a deep breath of relief. Her life was about to return to normal. "Thank you, Father. I assure you, I'm up to the task."

While the others took their time gathering their belongings and meandering out of the boardroom, Penny scooped up her portfolio, hiked her bag onto her shoulder, and made a beeline for the door. She paused as she passed behind Timothy, still stiffly seated in his tall-backed leather chair, and leaned in just close enough for him to hear her say, "The bitch is back."

She should have that printed on a T-shirt. It could be her new motto. *Oh, on stationery!* Personalized parchment with her name in glittery letters at the top and her new tagline scrolled across the bottom. It certainly would grab one's attention. Penny entertained the fantasy as she floated down the hallway to the elevator bay. She was in such a good mood, she kept right on going and took the stairs instead of waiting with the pack of suits who had also just left the meeting. Why *shouldn't* she feel like she was on top of the world? She counted off the happy in her life as her heels click-clacked down the cement steps of the stairwell. She had her job back. Her father had been pleased with her scouting Scott for head of security. She had hooked Scott up with a much-needed job. *And* she had a romantic night to look forward to with an extremely sexy woman. She still had a surprise or two up her sleeve for Lauren.

She pushed through the steel door to exit the stairwell into the lobby of the casino, grinning at the vision in her mind of the night ahead. Maybe she would even wear that new little red lace…

Penny stopped in her tracks and her stomach flip-flopped from excitement to shock at the sight across the casino lobby. There was Lauren, standing right there in the entrance to the casino, but she wasn't alone. She was with a woman Penny recognized from the photos on Lauren's computer. A woman who was supposed to be half a country away—Carolyn.

Carolyn, Lauren's ex, was there in Las Vegas in the lobby of the Rothmoor. Penny's throat went dry and pinpricks of panic played at her temples. She placed a hand against the wall for support and took a deep breath to steady herself.

Carolyn had come all the way from Chicago to find Lauren. There could only be one reason for that—she wanted Lauren back. A big romantic gesture like that might have an impact. Would Lauren really be swayed by it? The women had been a couple for so long before they broke up. Years. Many years. Lauren might be able to forgive and forget. Maybe Lauren just needed time to cool off. Maybe she got that time while they were on vacation and now getting back with Carolyn would be the easy thing to do. After all, once Lauren returned to Chicago, Penny would be out of sight, out of mind. A complete nonfactor in Lauren's life.

The sting of tears burned Penny's eyes. She had to get out of that lobby before Lauren realized Penny had seen them together. She turned the corner to the elevator bay on the lodging side of the lobby and made a dash for the first available car to arrive. Only after she was inside with the doors shut did she feel safe enough to release a breath of relief. Lauren had a whole life in Chicago. Penny had to accept that, no matter how deeply it was going to hurt her to watch Lauren go.

CHAPTER TWENTY-ONE

Lauren sat at the bar and traced her finger through the condensation on her wineglass. The shock of running into Carolyn in the lobby was still present like a chill in her veins, a shiver she couldn't shake. She had ducked out of the Rothmoor and taken refuge at Game of Flats in hopes of avoiding any further contact with Carolyn. She took a sip of her pinot grigio and waited for the muscles in her shoulders to unclench.

It wasn't just that Carolyn had shown up in Vegas, unexpected and unannounced. It wasn't even the temper tantrum Carolyn threw while threatening Lauren about using the photos of her. It was the twisting and the turning and Carolyn's attempt to manipulate Lauren's emotions. It had been so obvious to her in the lobby. Had it always been that way, a matter of manipulation between them? Was that all their whole relationship had ever been? The hurt that those questions still inspired was what was eating her. Disgusting her. The very reason why she was one hundred percent certain she would never again trust Carolyn. The love she once had for her had drained out of her the day

Carolyn walked out the door. The feeling still echoing in her heart now was shame for what a fool she had been to believe in that love in the first place.

She drained the last of the wine in her glass hoping to wash those feelings down. She wanted to be rid of the whole weirdness of seeing Carolyn before she headed back to the casino to meet Penny in her suite. It had been a big day for Ms. Penelope Rothmoor, businesswoman, and if everything had gone as planned, they should be celebrating for the rest of the night. Penny deserved that, and Lauren wasn't about to let anything put a damper on it, especially not some weird vibe brought on by seeing her ex. Lauren had to shake it off.

"You're drinking alone?" The vaguely familiar voice snapped Lauren back to reality as Jenna appeared behind the bar.

"Fancy meeting you here." Lauren smiled, glad for the friendly face.

"Yeah, my shift's just starting. I've got the whole night in front of me here." She grabbed the bottle of pinot and filled Lauren's empty glass. "Any word from Penny yet?"

"No. I thought maybe you or one of the other girls had heard something."

"Nothing on my end." Jenna gave a lopsided grin. "I think you'll be the first one she wants to tell. The rest of us will have to wait until tonight to get the scoop."

"Me?" Lauren couldn't imagine that Penny wouldn't go to her best friend, her friend circle, her usual network, with good news first.

"Yeah, you. You worked with her on the project. You helped her to put it all together. Plus…" Jenna shrugged. "…you know."

"I know?"

"She's pretty into you if you hadn't noticed."

A warmth spread through Lauren that had nothing to do with the alcohol she had consumed. The affirmation from Jenna meant a hell of a lot. There was no doubt that she and Penny were great together. It was obvious from the fireworks that went off inside of her when they touched. She had never connected with anyone as deep and fast as she had with Penny.

"Don't worry." She covered Jenna's hand with her own. "I'm pretty into her as well. The way she bounced back from this work thing, the way she's bold enough to go after what she wants...She's incredible. Honestly, I've never met anyone like her. And she brings out things in me that I'd totally forgotten were in there. Like my sense of humor. We laughed so hard telling each other stories when we were on vacation. Laughed until we cried. We egged each other on so much." She paused noticing the way Jenna had raised an eyebrow at her. "I'm sorry. I guess I was rambling there a bit."

"No need to apologize." Jenna shook her head. "It seems like you two are a perfect match."

"A perfect match that has been taking a break from regular, everyday life. Lives we will have to return to. Putting an end to the perfect."

Jenna took a long draw on her bottle of water as if thinking something through before speaking again. "People have been known to compromise for love, you know."

She smiled. It sounded so simple. *Compromise.* But life was never simple. And love rarely was either. "My life is in Chicago. I have a business there. It's where I belong. Just like how Vegas is where Penny belongs. I saw her face today when she was dressed in her suit and ready to shake up the casino world. I would never want to take that away from her."

"But you *do* love her?"

She held in her breath—and the truth. She hadn't had this conversation with Penny yet, and she certainly wasn't about to have it with Jenna, a woman she barely knew. Unfortunately, based on the burning heat in her cheeks, she suspected the answer was written on her face anyway. Everything about this situation made her feel like a teenager—tongue-tied, twisted up, heartsick, and giggly all at once. She took a sip of wine to stall for time.

Jenna laughed and sucked down more water. "You don't have to answer me. I have a terrible habit of butting in on my friend's business. I really shouldn't."

"It's okay," she finally managed. "I get it. I admire how much you all look out for each other."

Jenna opened her mouth as if to comment further, but quickly closed it when a new patron settled onto a stool at the other end of the bar and waved to ask for service.

"Saved by the bell, so to speak." Lauren shrugged and grinned, truly relieved for the excuse to change the subject.

Jenna's eyebrows scrunched together as she studied Lauren's face. "You know, I meant what I said that first night we met. We would love to have your work at the gallery. There is a home for you here in Vegas if you want it."

As Jenna moved down the bar to take care of her other customers, Lauren considered her words. All this time she had been so sure that Chicago was her life, but after her run-in with Carolyn she was starting to wonder if maybe Chicago was her *past*. She no longer had a lover there and she didn't really have friends there either. It was becoming more and more clear to her that art was the only thing she had in Chicago. And if Jenna's gallery gave her the opportunity to bring her art to the place where her lover and friends were, why not have it all?

Lauren leaned back against the round brass railing of the elevator car and watched the numbers slowly crawl up. She sucked in a deep breath and counted beats as she exhaled, anxious to get back to the suite and hear about Penny's day. She felt silly for not going immediately up when she finished with Carolyn. But it was her conversation with Jenna that had finally helped her shake off her funk. That thing she'd said about Penny being into her made Lauren's heart soar. Even with their complicated situation, it was still nice to know her feelings were reciprocated. Jenna said Penny would want to deliver any good news to her before anyone else, and that was the highest compliment Lauren had received in quite a while. Plus now that her return to Chicago had been reframed, Lauren was refueled by the possibility of moving her life to Las Vegas.

As the doors slid open to deposit her onto the fourteenth floor, Lauren resolved to revisit the conversation with Penny about relocating and giving this thing between them a real try. But for the night, celebrating Penny's success was her top priority. She would make the night as special as she possibly could for Penny's sake. There would be plenty of time to discuss the future later.

She let herself into the suite, expecting to be greeted by one very happy Penny. She even fixed a smile on her face so she would be ready to join right in on the revelry. But instead, when she walked through the door, she found complete silence.

"Penny?" she called out as she set her purse and camera on the counter of the kitchenette and made herself at home. She poked her head in the fridge and grabbed a bottle of water. Between the excitement of the afternoon and the wine, she was due for a little rehydration. "Where are you?"

A rattling came from the bedroom, indicating Penny was in the back of the suite. By the time Lauren made it into the living room, Penny was ambling down the hallway wrapped in a towel apparently fresh out of the shower. "Hey there."

"Hey yourself." Lauren took her by the hand and pulled her close. "Give me the good news."

Penny studied her face for a moment as if regarding her for the first time. Finally a smile slowly unfurled across her face. "Success!"

Lauren let out a whoop and wrapped her arms around Penny spinning her around. "I'm so proud of you. I knew you could do it. I can't wait to hear all about it."

Penny put her hands on either side of Lauren's head and pressed her mouth to hers. It was a long, slow, hungry kiss, indicating the mood for the night ahead of them. "And I can't wait to tell you over dinner. But if we don't get a move on we're going to be late for our reservations."

"You mean you're not wearing this tonight?" she teased as she tugged at the edge of Penny's towel.

"Maybe if you're lucky I'll put it back on later."

Penny in nothing but a towel, her damp hair framing her face, with the glow of success about her was one hell of a vision. A drop of water rolled down her bare shoulder. Lauren bit her lip in an effort to resist the urge to lick it off. Her pussy clenched at the thought of what they would do later that night and her core tingled with the beautiful thrill of anticipation. Business Penny was hot as fuck, even without the suit.

"Trust me." Lauren grinned and raised her eyebrows suggestively. "I plan on getting very lucky tonight."

CHAPTER TWENTY-TWO

Penny stood at the tall cocktail table in Game of Flats surrounded by her friends. The beat of the music thumped and echoed in her ribs. She had a pleasant buzz all through her that was partly due to the tequila shots Mara had insisted they throw back to toast her success, but mainly caused by the joy of being with all of her favorite people.

The sick feeling in her stomach brought on by seeing Lauren talking to Carolyn in the lobby that had hit her so strongly earlier had all but faded away. She had returned to her suite after seeing them together a quivering heap of nerves. Probably a combination of the shock of the sight on top of the adrenaline rush from the meeting with her father and the board. Her first instinct had been to sit and simmer. Have a glass of whiskey and be sitting in wait when Lauren returned. She would be ready to confront her the moment she walked through the door.

But after a few sips of alcohol and a few more deep breaths, she came to a realization: she had no good reason to be upset with Lauren for talking to her ex. Penny didn't have any claim on Lauren at all. Lauren had been very clear that she believed returning to their own lives was the best choice for the both of them and Penny had agreed. In a matter of days Lauren would be back in Chicago and whether or not she got back together with Carolyn at that point was beyond Penny's control.

She could, however, control how she used the time before Lauren left. She would pick herself up, celebrate her business win, and enjoy her time with this gorgeous woman. And maybe before their time together was over she could convince Lauren to choose her over Carolyn and stay.

The music shifted gears as the deejay slid into an old-school nineties slow jam. Hayleigh put her hands above her head and began a series of sexy body rolls, and Jenna, who had come out from behind the bar to join the celebration, danced up behind her. The others at the table hooted at the pair, encouraging Jenna to ramp her moves to serious grinding against her girlfriend.

Lauren leaned closer to Penny, and her sticky tequila breath tickled her ear. "I don't know if I can compete with that, but I would like to dance with you. Shall we?" She gestured toward the dance floor.

Penny followed Lauren's lead and they joined the throng of bodies moving to the beat-heavy song. Lauren had a way of making her feel like a princess, like someone who was special and living in a dream. As Lauren took her in her arms and swayed in time with the music, Penny's heart took flight. Lauren gazed at her with such an adoring expression, she truly felt like the belle of the ball. She knew fairytales weren't real, but in moments like this with Lauren, she at least felt they were possible.

The first song eased into a second, and Lauren twirled her around the dance floor again before pulling them together. Penny could feel Lauren's heartbeat against her. With a sigh, she rested her head on Lauren's shoulder, wishing the dance would go on forever.

Lauren planted a tender kiss on the top of her head. "I can feel you smiling against my neck. I never want to let you go."

"Then don't," Penny breathlessly murmured back, but as she did, the music shifted again and her words were lost in record scratches and electronic drums. As she followed Lauren back to their cocktail table, she willed herself to be brave enough to say the words again later when she could be heard loud and clear.

Hours later, back in her suite, Penny lay in Lauren's arms with her heart so full of contentment and love, she thought she would burst. She had suspected for a while what her true feelings were regarding the auburn-haired beauty tangled in the sheets beside her, but when Penny left that meeting earlier in the afternoon, she had known it for sure. It was obvious in the way she wanted to tell Lauren about her work victory before she shared it with anyone else. And it was the reason she had panicked when she saw Lauren talking to Carolyn in the lobby of the casino.

She was in love with Lauren Hansen.

As she basked in the afterglow of their lovemaking, she tried to block the image of Lauren and her former lover out of her mind. It was none of her business why Carolyn had come all the way to Vegas, or what the two of them had been discussing. All she knew for certain was it gave her a sour sensation in her stomach. The more she thought about it, the more that sour feeling turned into a burning, and before she could help herself she blurted out the truth. "I saw you and Carolyn together earlier in the lobby."

An uncomfortable silence stretched between them as Lauren pulled back from their cozy embrace. After propping herself up on one elbow, she finally spoke. "Why didn't you say something before?"

Penny shrugged and sucked her bottom lip between her teeth. She didn't want to cry and ruin the magical night they shared. "We were celebrating and having a good time. I didn't want to spoil it by being jealous." She sunk down into the sheets. The burning in her stomach had shifted to a quiver of embarrassment. Jealous and selfish was exactly how she had acted by bringing the topic up.

"I promise there's nothing to be jealous of at all." Lauren reached over and ran her hand through Penny's hair, brushing it away from her face. "Carolyn blindsided me by showing up here, and I made it perfectly clear that I wasn't interested in getting back together with her. It didn't matter to me what she said, I wasn't changing my mind on that."

Getting back together with her. The worst that Penny had imagined was true—Carolyn had come after Lauren to try to get her back. Hearing it was worse than not knowing. She should have never brought it up in the first place. "You know what? I shouldn't have said anything. It's none of my business."

"Penny, please listen to me. Carolyn and I are done for good. We have been for a while."

She rolled onto her side turning her back to Lauren. "It's okay. You don't have to explain anything to me. It's been a big day. I'm tired and I just need to get some sleep."

Lauren put a gentle hand on her shoulder. "Are you sure you're okay? You know, I've been thinking—"

"Really." Penny cut her off. There was no way she was actually going to sleep, but she didn't want Lauren to feel obligated to soothe away her jealousy. "We don't have to talk about it anymore. Goodnight."

CHAPTER TWENTY-THREE

Lauren leaned back into the corner of the L-shaped couch and took a sip of her coffee. She pressed into the bed pillow supporting her back and blew out a deep breath. She had tried to sleep after her conversation with Penny the night before, but long after Penny drifted off to sleep, she continued to toss and turn. She spent the better part of the night on the couch and at the first sign of sunrise, she had given in and propped herself up on caffeine.

She had wanted to tell Penny about the discussion with Jenna at the bar and the possibility of getting her work into a gallery in Las Vegas, but their night had taken such a weird turn. Penny had dropped a real bombshell when she mentioned seeing Carolyn in the lobby of the Rothmoor. At first Lauren thought telling Penny about Jenna's suggestion would help the situation, but then she decided they'd had enough drama for the night. Sitting in the light of dawn she was glad she had held back. It was best to get the details worked out and make sure it was a real possibility before she got Penny all excited about the prospect. It just wasn't fair to play with her heart like that. She still had enough time in Las Vegas to figure things out. After all, moving halfway across the country was a big leap of faith both professionally and personally.

She'd never imagined it would be this hard to say goodbye to Penny. It had been hard enough when their week in Hawaii was up, but now that they had spent this time together in Las Vegas, it was like she was leaving a piece of her heart behind. She was starting to think that maybe she didn't have to.

She sighed again, a deep, long breath that seemed bigger than the fresh, sunny morning should warrant. She wiggled off the couch, holding her mug high to keep her coffee from spilling. The sun streamed in through the French doors leading to the balcony that beckoned her.

Out in the warm heat of the morning, she took in the view of the city below. It was a lot more Glitter Gulch than Sin City. The rising sun reflected off the magnificent hotels along the strip in a brilliance that rivaled the sparkling lights and neon signs that ruled the night. The air was humming with heat already. It was going to be another scorcher.

She could picture herself living in Vegas. There was plenty of photo inspiration out here in the Entertainment Capital of the World. Plenty of stories to be told. And she could see herself with Penny, hitting the town dressed to the nines, enjoying the quiet times side by side, going to Sunday brunch every week with the girls. Falling into the rhythm of life with her.

But there was the whole other part, what she would be leaving in Chicago, and the hustle to develop contacts in a new town. Her regular patrons back home were more likely to move on to the next big thing to blow into the Windy City than to continue to seek her out from several states away. God only knew what the competition would be like in Vegas. She would be breaking into a whole new scene, all the vendors, venues, clients completely developed from scratch. And what about James? Would she ever be able to find another assistant who could live up to the standard he had set?

But waking up next to Penny every morning would be damn sweet, and a hell of a trade-off.

"You're up early." Either Penny had slipped onto the balcony with the stealth of a ninja, or Lauren had been so lost in her thoughts that she had been oblivious to her surroundings.

"I had a little trouble sleeping."

"About that." Penny came up behind her and wrapped her arms around Lauren. She rested her chin on her shoulder. "I'm sorry about last night. I should have never brought up the whole Carolyn thing. I guess I was a little jealous seeing the two of you together, and I just feel so immature for acting that way. I'm sorry." The look in her eyes was heartbreaking. She could be so hard on herself.

"Don't apologize. I should have told you I ran into her in the first place. I just didn't want to put a damper on our celebration."

Penny planted a sweet kiss on the curve of Lauren's neck. "Can we pretend the whole thing never happened and go back to the original plan of enjoying our time here together while it lasts?"

"I'd like that." Lauren set her mug down on the glass and wrought iron table beside them and faced Penny. She placed her hands on her upper arms and gave them a gentle squeeze before kissing her forehead, nose, and lips. "I'd like that very much. Look at that beautiful city out there. Let's go explore it together."

Penny turned her gaze to the edge of the balcony. "It is a hell of a view from up here, isn't it? You should see it by helicopter." Her mouth formed a little O and she grabbed Lauren's hand, apparently struck by inspiration. "That's what we should do today—a helicopter tour. I'll just make a couple calls and get it set up."

Lauren couldn't help but smile at her enthusiasm. She was relieved to see Penny bouncing back to her old take-charge self. "You'll just *make a couple calls* and get us a helicopter?"

"Hey." Penny shrugged and her eyes twinkled with teasing. "Being the daughter of a casino family does get *some* things handed to me on a silver platter. Let me just find my phone and I'll call."

"Use mine," Lauren offered as she followed Penny back into the suite. "It's right there on the counter."

"Thanks." Penny picked up the device and a frown immediately troubled her face. "Lauren, have you seen this? You have about a million messages from James."

"From James?" It was damn early in the Central Time Zone. There was no good reason for him to be trying to reach her at that hour. Something had to be wrong. "Let me see." There were numerous texts in addition to the missed calls, but every message was some variation of the same theme. *Call me ASAP.* "This can't be good."

Lauren poked at the screen to redial James's number. Her heart drummed in her chest. What hell could Carolyn have unleashed after being rejected in the lobby of the Rothmoor? That had to be the reason for James being so desperate to reach her. As the call picked up she braced herself for the worst.

"Hello!" James's chipper voice sing-songed through the line.

"James, my God, why are you blowing up my phone? Is everything okay there?"

"Everything is absolutely fabulous. I just need you to get your ass on the first flight back."

She nearly dropped her phone. She sucked in a deep breath and collected herself. "Do you mean today?"

"Lauren, the Hagan has given us the green light to go back in the building, and if we work our asses off, we can be ready to open next Thursday night."

"That's one week from today!" She rubbed her left temple with her free hand. She still needed to finish the new pieces she was adding to the show, and they had to completely redo the displays based on what James had told her earlier in the week. Then there was the promo that needed done…"How on Earth are we going to open a show in one week? No one will even know it's happening."

"Relax." His voice was silky smooth and full of confidence. A man with a plan. "We're going to sell opening night as an underground event. Only those in the know will know. Make it hip to be in on the secret."

It was pure genius and evidence that James was worth every single penny she paid him. A good assistant was hard to find, but he had never let her down. Hearing that he had a solid plan to make it happen, her heartbeat sped up. The adrenaline had begun to flow with the phrase *opening night*. Pure excitement at the idea of diving back into her work. "James, that's a fantastic idea. This could really work."

"So, you'll be back today?"

His question rang in her ears as she gazed across the suite at Penny, who was trying her best to look busy in her kitchenette. She delicately lifted some discarded mail, a scented candle and a ballpoint pen and wiped at the counter. She clearly had one ear on the phone call.

Lauren's instinct had been to drop everything and hightail it back to Chicago, but when she saw Penny across the room haphazardly distracted and beautiful all the same, her heart sank. This was not good news for Penny. Instead of a sightseeing tour of Vegas by helicopter, they would be saying goodbye. It was the end game they had been expecting, and yet somehow it was not playing out as they had expected at all.

"I'll be back today," Lauren confirmed and clicked off the call.

Lauren hung up and stared at her phone like she was an actress on a soap opera. Penny had only heard one side of the conversation, but it was enough to get the gist of it. Lauren was needed back in Chicago ASAP. She snapped her fingers, breaking up the silence that had settled over the suite in the wake of the phone call. "Hey, what are you doing? We've got to get you packed."

Lauren shook her head and blinked her eyes. It looked like she was waking from a trance. "No. What about our plans for the day? The helicopter tour. You were just about to call and make it happen."

"We'll do it the next time you're in town." She grabbed Lauren by the arm and marched her into the bedroom. "Come on. Grab your bag from the closet. I'll start looking up flights."

"You know, we could still do the helicopter thing." Lauren hauled her suitcase up onto the bed and started tossing clothes in while she talked. "I can get a flight later tonight or even first thing tomorrow."

Penny wheeled around on her heel, still poking at her phone screen. Lauren was moving around the edge of the bed, grabbing items as she went. Penny shook her head as Lauren bent down and grabbed the bra and panties that had been tossed to the floor the night before when they got back from the club. She sure had made herself at home in the suite in the short time she had stayed. Penny bit her lip to keep her focus on getting Lauren back to Chicago. She couldn't get all mushy now. "Absolutely not. If you have a chance to get the show open in a week you have to go for it. This is important. The damn helicopter can wait."

"Ah, businesswoman Penny again. I like that, but I'm serious." Lauren paused her frantic packing and a frown compromised her otherwise beautiful face. "I feel bad about running out on you like this. We had plans."

"Sometimes plans change. I understand that." Penny continued to scroll through the flight schedule on her phone, mostly to keep the momentum going. If she stopped to think about how her heart was breaking at the prospect of saying goodbye, she would lose it. She had to just keep moving. For Lauren's sake. "Okay. There's a ten-o-six that you can totally still make. If that doesn't work for some reason, there's a noon flight we can get you on. I'm booking it and ordering a car to pick you up."

Lauren placed her hands on Penny's shoulders as if to get her full-on attention. Her voice was quiet, almost a whisper. "I want you to know how much I appreciate all of this. I feel like a whole new woman compared to the one who left Chicago two weeks ago."

"Truth is, I do too." She bit the inside of her cheek to ward off the threatening tears. Her effort wasn't helped any by the dampness she saw collecting on Lauren's lashes. She shook her head to rattle the emotion away. They had said they weren't going to do a mushy goodbye. This was the way it had to end. "And I just know you're going to knock it out of the park with your show. That reminds me. I have something for you." Penny peeled away from Lauren and dug through the top drawer of her dresser until she found what she was looking for. Once she had it, she took Lauren's hand and transferred the plastic chip to her palm.

Lauren's eyebrows shot up when she realized what she had been given. "Your lucky chip?"

"*Your* lucky chip. Now we both have one." Penny grinned. "But don't worry, I rubbed them together to guarantee they are both lucky."

"You shared your luck with me?"

"Of course I did. I…" Penny stopped herself. She and Lauren had said all along this was how it would be. When it was time for Lauren to go back, that was it. Lauren had a job to do, and Penny wanted to be supportive, not make it harder for her to leave. This wasn't the time for grand declarations. She needed to reel her feelings in and be strong for the both of them. "I want your show to be a success." Tears finally spilled over as Penny held back the words she really wanted to say.

Lauren pulled her into a tight hug. "Thank you for understanding."

Penny sniffed and blinked hard. On the outside she might be the picture of strength and support, but on the inside she didn't understand why they were saying goodbye at all.

The bellhop came and loaded Lauren's bags onto a cart while the women stared at each other in the doorway. Penny chewed on her bottom lip and swiped at the dampness under her eyes. She wanted to say out loud every wild thought that was swirling inside her. The pained look on Lauren's face kept her from saying anything at all.

Lauren finally broke the silence. "I'll call you when I get in. We can email and text. We'll talk all the time. I want to hear every detail of your triumphant return to the casino."

"Every detail," Penny repeated dumbly as she forced a brave smile onto her face. "I promise."

Lauren blinked against her own tears as she wrapped her arms around Penny one last time and tenderly kissed her lips. "You take care of yourself."

Penny nodded, unable to speak without completely breaking down. Lauren slipped out of her embrace. She sucked in her breath and watched helplessly as Lauren started down the hall after the bellhop. If she turned and looked back, her heart was sure to shatter into a million pieces, but if she didn't look back, it would somehow hurt even worse. Without waiting to find out which way it would be, she shut the door and let Lauren go. They had said it time and time again—going back to their separate lives was what was best. It made sense. But as Penny slumped to the floor, heart aching and tears flowing like they might never stop, none of it made any sense to her at all.

Lauren sat in her plump, comfortable first-class seat on the plane and tipped her forehead to the window. The gray tarmac below offered neither comfort for her stirring soul nor answers to the debate going on in her heart. A strange sensation swirled in her middle. She was excited to get back to work and see her project through, but there was a melancholy at leaving Penny behind. She had become accustomed to not only spending her days and nights with the woman, but doing so in almost constant close quarters. Leaving Las Vegas was going to be a shock to her system.

She reached into her jacket pocket and pulled out the plastic five-dollar chip Penny had given her. She twirled it between her fingers as the plane began to roll forward for takeoff. They had left a lot of things unsaid and they both knew it. It was for the best. They both had professional lives that needed their attention, and that was just the way it was. Lauren settled back in her seat, dizzy from the runway speeding by below her. She clicked her thumbnail along the ridges on the edge of her lucky chip. It was for the best.

"Ma'am, your pinot grigio." The flight attendant delivered a plastic cup of wine, putting Lauren out of her thoughts.

She took a sip and blew out a long breath. Photo proofs on her tablet that James had emailed over right after their phone call earlier needed reviewed, but her heart wasn't quite in it yet. Instead, she took another drink of wine and closed her eyes as a tear slid down her cheek. She pictured herself back on the beach with Penny by her side, waves crashing in the distance, their fingers touching on the armrest of their lounge chairs. She would be buried in work soon enough. Until she stepped off the plane she would remain one of the vacation people.

CHAPTER TWENTY-FOUR

Penny sat in the beams of sunlight shining through the picture window in the front of Café Gato, absentmindedly stroking the warm fur of the large orange cat sunbathing on the window seat.

It was Thursday, which meant a couple thousand miles away in Chicago it was opening night for Lauren's show. She was probably putting the finishing touches on things, sending James running on last-minute errands, assembling her outfit for the night. Maybe she was getting her nails and hair done. She always looked so sophisticated with her hair swept up in an up-do, long duster earrings hanging down, her neck exposed and completely kissable.

Penny had been plagued by memories and fantasies about Lauren since the day she left. Seven days later, she was still flip-flopping between melancholy and frustration. She had talked to Lauren every day, but the conversations were clipped, abbreviated versions of the kind they had become accustomed to during their time together. Between Lauren rushing to complete everything she needed to for the opening and Penny getting back into her usual management duties at the Rothmoor, they were lucky to get more than a few sentences in, and that was when they were able to even get their schedules to match at all.

Lauren had invited Penny out to Chicago for opening night, but she had declined. As much as she yearned for Lauren's touch, her company, the ability to hold an entire conversation without one of them having to run off to verify a proof or monitor gaming table losses, she just couldn't put herself through it. She was all too familiar with the pain of saying goodbye to Lauren after the joy of being together. She couldn't risk the heartbreak all over again for a few hours of pleasure. No, she would pass on this visit and maybe try it another time when her heart had had time to heal and the feelings had faded. If the feelings faded.

"Yoohoo, Penny." Mara waved her hand between Penny and the window. "You know me and Frankie are sitting at this table too, right? You have got to snap out of this."

"Yeah, girl," Frankie chimed in between sips from her mug. "Breakup Penny is a very sad Penny. Maybe we need a night out at the Flats."

"Right." Mara rolled her eyes. "I swear Frankie will do anything to feast her eyes on that deejay at Game of Flats."

"I'm not going to Flats tonight, and I'm not Breakup Penny." She frowned and Singe the orange cat slinked out of her reach, as if sensing the shift in her mood from glum to annoyed. "We didn't break up. We weren't even together."

"You weren't together?" Mara scrunched up her face and threw a balled-up paper napkin in her direction. "That's total crap. You and Lauren were totally together."

"I don't know what the hell we were." She shook her head. "For all I know, she went back to Carolyn the minute she got back into Chicago."

"Now *that's* total crap." Frankie furrowed her brow in concern and pushed a muffin across the table in Penny's direction. "You better eat something, sweetie. You're talking crazy. Maybe your blood sugar is low."

Penny shook her head at the offered treat. She had been wrestling for days with how much to tell her friends about seeing Carolyn and Lauren in the lobby of the Rothmoor. On the one hand, she could use their support and their confirmation that she was overthinking the subject. On the other, she was embarrassed that she had fallen hard for and was now sitting around missing a woman who had possibly returned to her ex. She ran her finger along the edge of her plate, eyes down, stalling for time while she made up her mind.

"What's that face?" Mara reached over to tip up her chin and forced their gazes to meet. "What aren't you telling us?"

Leave it to Mara to ferret out the truth and call her out on it. Mara knew Penny better than anyone, and she wasn't exactly the *let it slide* type.

"I didn't tell you guys before because I felt so stupid. But after my meeting with the board last week I saw Lauren in the lobby talking to her ex, Carolyn."

"Oh, damn," Frankie muttered.

"Hold up. Jenna and Lauren hung out at Flats that afternoon, remember? They mentioned it when we were celebrating your return to work. I'm sure if Carolyn had been there too Jenna would have said something to one of us." Mara chewed her lip as if concentrating hard enough to add it all up. "Even if you did see them in the lobby, Lauren must not have spent too much time with her. What time were you in the lobby?"

"It was around three thirty. Maybe four."

"So they didn't spend much time together at all," Frankie summed up, her tone slightly triumphant.

"But that's not really the point," Penny argued with a heavy sigh. "It doesn't matter if she spent two minutes with her or all damn day. Lauren was talking to her ex. Her ex who had come all the way here from Chicago to find her. And now Lauren is back in Chicago where Carolyn is, and I'm here. It makes sense that the whole reason Carolyn came to Vegas was to get Lauren back."

"Is that what Lauren said she came here to do?" Frankie reached across the table and grabbed Penny's hand.

Penny dropped her gaze to the table and focused on the gold flecks in the pale lime Formica. "Yes."

At her friends' stunned silence, Penny pulled away from Frankie's touch. She leaned back in her chair and crossed her arms in front of her body. Her temples were starting to throb with frustration. Maybe blabbing about her deep dark fears had been a mistake "Lauren said she told Carolyn to get lost, and she kept telling me that the two of them had been over for good for a long time. I don't have any reason not to believe her. Hell, I shouldn't have even asked her about it in the first place. She didn't owe me anything. Like I said, we weren't together."

"Would you cut that shit?" Mara asked loudly enough to draw some stares from surrounding tables. She scrubbed at her face with her hands and took a deep breath before leaning in closer and lowering her voice. "Lauren was totally in love with you."

Penny couldn't stop her jaw from dropping. "She told you she was in love with me?"

"She didn't have to tell me." Mara shrugged. "It was written all over her face anytime I saw the two of you together."

Penny shook her head. "Then why didn't she stay? I even offered to get her space at the Rothmoor to set up and display her photography, but she shot it down. She said it wasn't the right kind of space to get her work seen."

"Why didn't you push the issue if you wanted her to stay?" Mara stuck out her chin and mimicked Penny's cross-armed pose, challenging her. "You could have come up with some other solution."

"She'd already said no. My pride was hurt, and I didn't want to make the situation harder than it already was. She had a show to open. She had to go. I didn't want to make it hurt even more than it already did."

"Then why didn't you offer to relocate to Chicago?" Frankie asked simply. "You love her, right?"

"Yes…I do." It was like the floor dropped out below her. Penny's stomach was in her throat like she had jumped up in a descending elevator car. The whole time she had focused on finding a way to keep Lauren in Vegas. She'd never even considered the possibility of moving to Chicago to be near her.

Her cheeks burned with embarrassment at how selfish that had been. Now that the idea had been presented, she found it quite exciting. She'd have to rework a couple of things, of course. "But I just got my job at the Rothmoor back. What will my father think if I tell him I'm going to leave?"

"You never lost that job, you were just on a break," Mara pointed out. "Besides, you don't really need your job at the Rothmoor. Your family's got more money than God. You'll get by fine even if you don't find a job in Chicago. And whether you work at the Rothmoor or not, you'll take over for your dad as owner one day."

Frankie nodded along in agreement. "You can always come back to Vegas."

Penny swallowed hard. Everything her friends were saying made sense, and she couldn't believe it took Lauren leaving for her to see it. She loved her job at the Rothmoor, but she also loved Lauren. There would be other jobs, but there was only one Lauren Hansen. "You're right. I should go to Chicago and be with her. What we had is worth giving it a shot."

Frankie let out a whoop and Mara pounded the table like she was sealing the declaration with the bang of a gavel.

Penny's pulse pounded hot like fire was moving through her veins. "What...what the hell do I do now?"

"You go to Chicago and get the girl!" Frankie raised her hands in the air like she was shaking pom-poms.

Penny looked between her two friends, as if her suddenly hopeful heart even needed a second opinion.

"I agree with Frankie." Mara gave a firm, encouraging nod. "All you've done since Lauren left is work and mope. I know you love Lauren, and I don't think you should wait another moment to tell her that you'll move to Chicago if that's what it takes to be with her."

"Her show opening is tonight. She invited me, but I told her I couldn't go."

"Fuck that. You're going." Mara scooted forward in her chair and started poking at the screen of her phone. "I'm checking flights to Chicago."

"Oh my god, this is going to be so romantic." Frankie clapped her hands together. "Do you have something to wear that is opening night appropriate?"

"Please. Have you seen her walk-in closet?" Mara laughed, never taking her eyes off her phone. "It's like fashion week on steroids in there."

"I know exactly what I want to wear, but I've got to get back and pack. And find a flight. And get my ass to the airport." Penny glanced at the clock and did the math in her head. "It's already almost noon in Chicago. The show starts at eight. I'll never make it."

"I've found you a flight." Mara stood up abruptly. "You're going to make it, but you better get your ass in gear. Come on, let's go."

CHAPTER TWENTY-FIVE

Lauren had started the day excited about opening night and ready to take on the world, but that evening as she stood in the foyer of the Hagan and did her last-minute check of guests on the door list, her heart sank. She had left Penny on the list despite her repeated declines of Lauren's numerous invites. Penny had cited getting back into the routine of work and not being able to take any days off as her main reasons for not flying out for the show, but Lauren feared there was really something else behind Penny not wanting to come to Chicago. Maybe Penny had accepted they were a vacation fling, nothing more, and if that was true, then it was time for Lauren to accept it too. The vacation was over, and so were they. The thought clawed at Lauren's heart and had been the reason for more than a few emotional breakdowns over the past week, but she was trying her best to make her peace with it.

She set down the clipboard with the list of will-call guests and pulled her phone out of her hip pocket. One more call inviting Penny to come wouldn't hurt. Persistence was a very powerful ally. Her fingers moved swiftly over the screen to pull up her contact info, but then she paused with her fingertip poised above Penny's name. The pause was just long enough for doubt to come creeping in.

Why?

Why make Penny create another excuse for not coming to Chicago? Why put yet another awkward conversation between them? Why put herself through any of it?

Accept it.

Lauren tucked her phone back in the pocket of her jeans, but signed off on the list as it was, leaving Penny's name on it. She could try to accept things the way they were, but that didn't mean she was ready to completely shut the door on hope.

"Time for the final walk-through!" James called from the main exhibit room. He had been his cheerful chipper self all morning long, a good balance to the dark cloud of a sullen mood that was hanging over her, and Lauren appreciated that.

She fixed a smile on her face and went to join him. This was her big day, and even if her heart was broken in two, she had a show to put on. She found everything was in place and the lighting would maximize the impact of the art. She had decided on stark white walls with the photographs framed against them. Some of the pieces were surrounded by striking black frames, some in brushed silver for a softer effect. Bump-outs built into the walls added dimension, and a friend of James who was a potter had created a line of opalescent black glazed pieces that were displayed on white columns peppered across the floor.

James made gentle approving noises as they stepped from one photo to the next, confirming that the affect they had intended had been achieved. One particular grouping caused him to actually pause for a moment as he admired the work.

"These pieces you added this week were a smart move." James gestured at the cluster of photos from Hawaii surrounding a larger one—the shot of Penny's reflection in the puddle. Although they were all black-and-white images, Lauren remembered distinctly how that red and white polka-dot dress danced and twirled as Penny moved. How it clung to her body in all the right places. How she peeled it off Penny right before they made love. James studied the cluster a beat longer before continuing. "I wouldn't be surprised if this piece was the biggest hit of the night."

They moved on to the display of life shots from Las Vegas and Lauren placed a worried palm against her cheek. "I hope this one goes over well. I feel like I'm kind of indulging myself."

"Are you kidding me?" He squinted at her. "I've never seen Las Vegas look so human. You've really given it a fresh face with these shots."

Lauren's mind was drawn back to the day she took the photos. It was the day Penny had presented her plan for the casino security team. And the day Carolyn had tracked her down. But it was also the day Jenna had offered to get her work into a Las Vegas gallery. If only she had had the time to follow up on that lead. If only she had said something to Penny about it before she left. If only…

"Any word from the inspiration for this addition to the show?" James's soft, concerned voice interrupted her thoughts. He placed his hand on Lauren's shoulder and gave it a comforting squeeze.

Instinctively she reached for her hip and touched her phone still safely in place in her pocket. She shook her head. "No. I'm afraid she won't be joining us tonight."

"Shame." He sighed and pulled her into a side-arm hug. "I'd really like to meet the woman who inspired you to produce this gorgeous display."

Lauren's stomach lurched and another ache pierced her heart. There was no way she could accept that these images were nothing more than a part of her past. She fought back tears as she sank into James's strong embrace, grateful to have him by her side for the show. It wasn't the first time since she had been back in Chicago that she realized what an asset her assistant was. Suddenly she had a thought that pushed the door to hope her heart refused to close even further open. "Do you think you could ever live there? In Las Vegas?"

James pulled back enough to meet her gaze, his expression thoughtful. "I'd be open to it if the right offer came along."

CHAPTER TWENTY-SIX

"You said you found me a flight. You said I'd make it on time." Penny zipped the carry-on bag that she had loaded to the gills with anything she might need for a one-night stay in Chicago. The adrenaline rush that had kicked in when she had decided to surprise Lauren had waned as she realized the holes in Mara's plan. "This is never going to work."

"First of all, you have to have faith." Mara took that bag and hoisted it onto her shoulder as she ushered Penny out of the suite and into the hallway. "Second, there's a car waiting for you out front, so move your faithless ass."

"I'm serious, Mara." Penny followed her to the elevator and dug through her purse for her lip gloss. "This flight won't get me there before the show starts. I'll be lucky to even land in Chicago before the show is over."

"That flight I booked you is just Step One. Your charm and powers of persuasion are the keys to making this work. Besides, there were no available spots left on the flight that would get you there on time. There was no other chance to get you to Chicago. We had to work with what was available."

It wasn't until they had rushed back to Penny's suite to pack, leaving Frankie to get back to work at the animal shelter, that Mara had revealed her plan to get Penny to the Windy City. Unable to book a flight at the last minute that arrived in time to make Lauren's show, Mara grabbed a first-class seat on a later flight. The idea was Penny would get to the airport early and attempt to find someone on the earlier flight who would be kind enough to swap with her. Mara was convinced this was a great idea. Penny was not quite as sure.

They weaved through the crowd in the lobby of the Rothmoor in silence, but once out front of the casino, Mara leaned over and kissed her best friend on the cheek. A warm but determined smile crinkled her eyes as she locked her gaze on Penny's. "You'll figure out a way to make this work. You'll find your way to Lauren. I know it." She handed off the overnight bag to the driver as Penny climbed into the back of the long, dark car.

"This is crazy." Penny looked up at her friend, who was holding the car door waiting for her to get settled in her seat. She couldn't believe she had agreed to go along with this half-baked plan.

"Love makes you do crazy things." Mara shrugged. "Make sure you text me when you get there. I'll want details."

"We'll see." Penny rolled her eyes, but a rush of fondness for her best friend ran through her. Only Mara would say something like that, and only Mara would have pushed Penny to take a chance and go after the woman she loved. "Hey, thanks for everything."

"You got it." Mara winked and closed the door, leaving Penny to face Step Two of the plan on her own.

Penny clutched her boarding pass in her fist and navigated through the travelers standing on the moving walkway that rolled along the center of the airport terminal. By the time she spotted Gate B37, her ribs had been elbowed three times, her foot had been run over by a rolling case, and she had been given more dirty looks than a whore in church. If she never said the phrase, "excuse me" again, it would be too soon.

She stood on the edge of the seating area and surveyed the crowd. Chatting people up buoyed by nothing more than blind optimism was not usually her style. It was much more of a Mara thing, like the wacky plans she used to drag Penny into when they were in college. Somehow Penny had felt more fearless back then. Sucking in a deep breath, she closed her eyes and pictured her reunion with Lauren when she finally made it to Chicago. In the front pocket of her jeans her fingertips troubled the plastic chip she had stuck in there before leaving her suite. She could be satisfied with what she had or she could take a chance. There was never such a literal interpretation as that moment when she stood with a boarding pass she didn't really want in her hand while overlooking a roomful of travelers who had the golden ticket she wanted. The lucky chip had spoken, but where to start?

There were a few families with young children and she ruled those out right away. Slim chance of having part of a family staying behind while the others went on. A good part of the crowd appeared to be retired travelers, those who had the freedom of schedule to fly in and out of town in the middle of the day midweek. She labeled them as "maybes." What she needed was a twenty-something singleton. Someone traveling with a group of friends. Someone who would be open to making a few bucks. Her gaze finally settled on a young woman with choppy, short blond hair, a flannel shirt tied around her waist, and an army-green backpack with a rainbow appliqué stitched on it slung over her shoulder. Bingo. Penny slipped her chip back into her pocket and went for it.

"Um, hi." She smiled brightly at the young woman as she approached. "I…uh… Are you on this flight to Chicago?"

The woman's face came to life as it registered that she was the object of Penny's inquiry. This was exactly the person Penny needed to run into, the power of queer community and all that. Time to employ the feminine wiles. She turned the charm up another notch.

"Oh, I love your boots." Penny fussed over the woman's Clarks and ushered her into a seat in the row of molded plastic chairs. "Did you buy them here in Vegas?"

The blonde shook her head and her shaggy locks flew about like they needed a moment to catch up to the rest of her. "No. I'm not from here. I've had them for a while. Super comfortable. I'm Nicky, by the way."

"Hi, Nicky." She reached out her hand to shake. Business habit. "I'm Penny. So, you're from Chicago? Heading home?"

"Yeah." Nicky flipped her hair out of her face with another whip of her head. "I was just in Las Vegas with…just for a few days."

"Perfect." Penny smiled and went in for the pitch. "I'm hoping you can help me out with something. You see, I need to get to Chicago today, as soon as possible. And I have a first-class ticket on a flight that leaves at four, but that flight won't get me there on time. I'm trying to make it to a show there."

"Oh!" Nicky interrupted and slapped a hand on Penny's thigh in her excitement. "What kind of show? A musical? *Hamilton* or something?"

"No, it's…it's not that kind of show. It's actually a—" Penny stopped herself with a shake of her head. She was getting way off track and wasting valuable time. She closed her eyes and took a deep breath to pull herself together. It was time to get on the get. "It's actually not the important thing here. The important thing is that there's this woman, and she's in Chicago. And we had a fling on vacation, but then we started to really get to know each other, and I ended up totally falling for her. Only I didn't realize I couldn't live without her until she was gone." She paused to finally take a breath. Nicky's gaze was trained on her as if hanging on every word of the drama. "I've got to get to her and tell her how I feel. I need to get on this flight, but it's full and I couldn't get a seat, but I do have a first-class ticket to Chicago that leaves later tonight, and I guess I was hoping that you would take pity on me and swap tickets."

Nicky seemed to startle out of her trance as Penny's words registered. She scrunched up her face as she added two and two together. "So you want me to give you my ticket?"

"Not give." Penny put her hand on top of Nicky's, which was still resting on her thigh. "*Trade*. For first class. And I'll pay for your meal here at the airport—whatever you want—while you're waiting for the flight."

Nicky's face softened. "You want my ticket so you can go declare your love to a woman? That is *so* romantic!"

Success! Penny had her hooked. She just needed to reel her in. This was it. She made a choice, she put herself out there, and she got the job done. She was practically on her way to Lauren. Nicky's eyes shone with sympathy and she was nodding her head. She just hadn't actually said the words that she would do it.

Penny pushed her along. "So what do you think? Will you trade?"

Nicky opened her mouth to answer, but before she got any words out, her eyes went wide at something over Penny's shoulder.

"Who the hell is this?"

A broad-shouldered woman with hair dyed jet black came to a halt directly in front of the pair. Her gray V-neck T-shirt stretched across her chest, the lines where her sports bra cut into her flesh underneath were clearly visible, and her faded denim jeans were ripped off and organically frayed just below the knees. Not quite capri length, not quite shorts. The chain that linked her wallet to her belt completed the message of the outfit: *I'm a mother fucking badass.* In her hands were two cups of coffee, but her wide-legged stance indicated that she was prepared to defend her ground should she be required to do so.

"Bianca, this is Penny," Nicky explained in a gentle, soothing tone of voice as if she was used to the art of calming the woman. She also slowly slid her hand from Penny's thigh, a motion that did not go undetected by the hotheaded Bianca.

"Oh no, I don't think so." Bianca set the paper coffee cups on the floor in an effort to free her hands. "Nicky's *my* girl. You need to step the fuck away from her right now."

Penny sprang up from her seat and took a giant step backward, away from the hot mess of a potentially verbally abusive relationship. "We were only talking. Nicky was trying to help me."

"Yeah," Nicky chimed in. "I was just trying to help. I can't help it if beautiful women are drawn to me. She was in distress, she saw me and instantly knew I was the solution. It's like a chemical thing. Natural, you know. Women see me and they want me."

"What?" Penny put even more distance between her and whatever was developing in front of her. She had no idea what Nicky was rambling on about, but by the way Bianca's expression flashed from anger to attraction, it was clear that Penny's part in the act was over. She had been merely a pawn in some weird game between Nicky and her girlfriend. Any thought of getting that plane ticket swap was vapor. Gone. The attempt had been a total bust.

Nicky and Bianca were tangling up in a passionate embrace and working up to a full-fledged makeout session as Penny turned away to leave. Head down in defeat, she shuffled back through the seating area searching out a quiet space to get her thoughts together and decide what to do next.

Such an epic fail. The trade for Nicky's ticket had seemed like a sure thing, but Penny hadn't been able to close the deal. Where was her business acumen when she needed it? She rubbed at her temples to rid her brain of that train of thought. If there was one thing she had proven over this whole adventure with Lauren, it was that business and matters of the heart were completely different animals.

Lauren. Penny had been so close to getting to her in time for the opening of the show, but suddenly it seemed like that was nothing more than a pipe dream. She still had her ticket for the later flight. She would make it to Chicago a little after ten o'clock local time. She had done the math in her head a million times. By the time she would grab a car from the airport to town, she wouldn't arrive at the Hagan until after the show was over. That was the plain and simple fact.

With a heavy sigh she checked her phone for the time. Less than twenty minutes left to convince someone to take pity upon her and swap out their tickets. It was a total long shot in the first place, on top of the fact that after the Nicky-Bianca experience she was more than a little hesitant to approach another stranger. Should she show up in Chicago with the spirit of *better late than never*, or should she just call it a day and go home? Maybe rework the plan with Mara and try again another time? Her stomach clenched and a sour feeling bubbled inside of her. Was this a sign that she and Lauren were not meant to be? Was it the signal to give up and let the whole thing go? She pressed her eyes shut, recognizing the swell of oncoming tears. There was no way she was going to stand there and cry in the middle of the airport. The experience itself had been humiliating enough already. Just as she was about to make a sprint for the ladies' restroom, she heard a gentle voice behind her.

"Excuse me, miss?"

Penny wheeled around to see an older man holding his hat in one hand, and holding out a handkerchief in the other. She attempted to fix a smile on her face and waved off the offering. "Oh, thank you. I'm okay though."

"If you're sure." He shrugged and tucked the linen square back into his pocket. "I couldn't help overhearing your plight back there. I'd like to help."

His words caught her off guard. She had been ready to nod politely and walk away, but then the last bit registered in her mind. Her jaw dropped and her feet froze in place. She shook her head, certain that she had misunderstood. "You...want to help me?"

The old man nodded once, sure in his statement. "I do. By the way, my name is Henry. I'm heading home after a stay with my daughter and grandchildren. It was my first visit since my wife passed away last fall. Bea and I were married for fifty-three years. We were blessed with a beautiful family and many happy years together." He shifted his weight, rocking from side to side as he spoke. "I heard you talking about the woman you love. You need to get to her, so please, take my ticket. I'm retired and in no rush to get home. There's no one waiting for me there. I'm not on this flight, but the one a couple of gates down. It leaves here at three and I don't know if that's any better than the ticket you have now, but if it is you're welcome to it. Go to your love."

A flight that left Vegas at three would land in Chicago at eight thirty and that should get her to the Hagan before Lauren's show ended. It wasn't perfect, but it was better than the ticket she had. She grabbed his hands in both of hers. It was a miracle. This man who had overheard her conversation, out of the kindness of his heart, was encouraging her to go after the woman she loved. If this wasn't a sign that she shouldn't give up, what was? She released him long enough to swipe a hand across her lashes, brushing off the happy tears that had sprung up. "Henry…thank you."

"Come on, young lady, we better get these tickets swapped before it's too late. You have a flight to catch."

CHAPTER TWENTY-SEVEN

By nine thirty, Lauren had hugged enough acquaintances and semi-strangers to last her a lifetime. It was funny how every single embrace had felt stiff and obligatory. Penny was the only person she wanted to hold in her arms. Lauren's cheeks hurt from smiling politely, and her feet hurt from standing in heels for hours, but the end of the event was in sight.

It was evident in the way some of the women in attendance greeted her that the word was out on Lauren and Carolyn's breakup. There had been a lot of hair flipping during conversation, light touches on the arm meant to convey interest, and batting of eyelashes from other parties. Lauren noticed these things and picked up on the signals, but only in an observing, almost clinical, way. None of it had stirred any emotion in her. None of it was Penny.

Overall, the night had been a success. That had been confirmed repeatedly through the smart glances she and James had shared as they mingled with the crowd. In spite of the quick turnaround between the date on which they had announced the opening and the actual night of the event, they had managed to nearly reach the gallery's capacity with attendance. His idea to go "underground" had worked. It was the hip place to be. Lauren had received compliment after compliment on her work, her vision, even her dress for the evening. But there was still something holding back perfection in her mind. Something was missing.

She grabbed a champagne flute from the tray of a passing waiter and worked her way across the floor one last time. The gallery was still full of beautiful people mingling, drinking, keeping the party going. Lauren hid her sigh behind a smile as she sipped her drink. She was ready to call it a night. She was pleased with the way the opening had gone, but she had realized something important, something she could no longer deny. Success was not fulfilling without the woman she loved. She needed Penny by her side.

She had been foolish to think leaving a ticket at the door and hoping for Penny's arrival would yield results. It had been Lauren's pride that had kept her from calling Penny and asking her again to fly out for the event. Damn, stupid pride. The same damn pride that had immediately turned her off when Penny had offered her space at the Rothmoor to have her next show. She could follow up on that lead Jenna had for her, and if that didn't work, she would find another gallery. Hell, if leaning on the Rothmoor until she got her feet under her in Las Vegas was what it took to have a life with Penny, then so what? Being with her was what she wanted more than anything. After their time apart, Lauren was certain of that. She could only hope it wasn't too late to tell Penny how she felt.

Dipping one finger under the neckline of her dress, Lauren plucked out the plastic chip she had tucked inside her bra earlier. She turned it over in her palm as she drained the last of the bubbly from her glass. In her mind she could hear word-for-word what Penny had said about her chip. *I can hold on to what I have or I can take a chance.* In a minute it would be time to give her thank-you speech. After that the show would be done. She would skip out on the after parties, decline the offers for nightcaps and celebratory shots. Instead she would take a chance and call Penny. She needed to tell her she wanted a real relationship with her, and if that meant relocating to Las Vegas and starting fresh in the art scene there then that was what she would do. She would tell Penny she was in love with her. It might be too late. Penny might reject her or say Lauren missed her chance. That was a risk Lauren was willing to take. It was a risk she *had* to take. She couldn't live not knowing if Penny still felt the same. Lauren had to take her shot, and she wouldn't put it off any longer than was absolutely necessary.

A light touch on her shoulder brought her focus back to the moment. She spun around to find James smiling brightly at her. "Ready for your big moment, starshine?"

She nodded resolutely, set her empty glass down on another passing tray, and followed James to the small platform they had set up in the corner of the gallery. Lighting that earlier had accentuated the photographs positioned on the wall now illuminated James as he called the partiers to attention and gave Lauren a gracious introduction. As the crowd welcomed her with applause, she joined James on the platform, kissed him on the cheek, and beamed out at the people gathered in the room. She fought the urge to squint into the lights as she began her speech.

"Hello, everyone, and thank you so much for joining us tonight. As with any work of art, blood, sweat, and tears went into every part of this show. But there was another element, the most vital element of all, that made these photographs what you see before you tonight." A swell of emotion built in her throat. It was completely true. Her art was a reflection of her experience, her being. The art she produced was a direct result of her feelings and the things that moved her. And deep down she knew her art was different—her *life* was different—for having loved Penny. She swallowed hard. She needed to make it through the speech so she could get out of there and reach out to Penny. She addressed the crowd again. "That element was love."

She took a deep breath to stall while she struggled to keep her emotions in check. Blinking to ward off tears, she raised her chin and scanned the crowd. All eyes were on her, the attendees hanging on her every word. It was truly her moment to shine, just as James had said. She had earned it. Lauren was proud of the work she had presented, and she was ready now to wrap up her speech and express her gratitude. She had opened her mouth to do just that when a flutter of activity at the entrance to the gallery caught her eye and made her pause. She blinked hard again, barely trusting that she was actually seeing what she thought she was seeing. *Who* she thought she was seeing.

There, at the very back of the crowd, under-dressed for the event in dark skinny jeans and a light pink linen jacket, and pulling a rolling carry-on case behind her, was Penny. Penny Rothmoor was in Chicago. She had come to Lauren's show even without a last-minute second-try invitation. And the way she was looking at Lauren—full of love and warmth and everything good they had shared between them—had to mean one thing.

Lauren couldn't hold back the beaming smile that spread across her face at the sight of the woman she loved. When Penny blew her a kiss and nodded encouragingly for her to continue her speech, the tears Lauren had attempted to staunch when she began finally spilled over. Happy tears fueled by love and joy and hope for a future with Penny.

Lauren cleared her throat and continued. "As I was saying, I've found inspiration in so many places lately, here in Chicago, in Hawaii, and particularly in Las Vegas." Heat rushed her cheeks as she shared a meaningful glance with Penny. She held her gaze as she went on. "And what it's led me to discover is the importance of being brave enough to take chances. It's something I'm committing to moving forward, and I hope my art will inspire all of you to take chances as well. It's been my pleasure to share tonight with each of you, and I thank you again for your support."

Applause broke out again as Lauren concluded her speech, but she only had one thing on her mind as she stepped down from the platform and moved through the crowd—getting to Penny. A buzz pulsed through her, propelling her forward. Her chest swelled with love and desire and her gaze remained locked on the beautiful face of the woman who had appeared as if out of her dreams. She didn't dare look away. She was far too afraid Penny would disappear and she would find it was all some kind of cruel illusion. As Lauren reached her and actually touched her with her own two hands, everyone else in the room seemed to drop away. It was as if they were the only two people in the world, much less the gallery. A tingle began at her scalp and moved to the back of her eyes as her lover's name came out in a gasp. "Penny…"

Penny dropped her bag and took Lauren in her arms. "God, I've missed you so much."

Lauren tasted the salty tears on Penny's skin as she kissed her cheek. Proof that she was real, not a figment of her imagination. "I've missed you too. I can't believe you're here."

"You wouldn't believe what I went through to get here. But having you in my arms was worth every minute of it." Penny blinked hard against the emotion spilling over her lashes. "After you left I just… My world wasn't the same. Everything's changed. I'm not right without you. We can live here or Vegas, or wherever the hell in the universe you want to live as long as we're together. I just want to be with you."

"I was a fool to think I could leave you behind and continue on like we never happened." Lauren choked back her own tears as she confessed the truth. "You're all I've thought about since I left Las Vegas. It was like I left a piece of my heart there. I need you, Penny." She put her lips softly against her cheek and nibbled her way across Penny's jaw until she found her lips. Her heart swelled as her mouth met Penny's in a strong, deep kiss that felt like coming home.

It was the kind of kiss that could have gone on forever, or at the very least, led to so much more, if only they weren't standing in the middle of a party in a crowded art gallery. Lauren longed to be alone with her once again and do their reunion properly, without a throng of onlookers. As their lips parted, she ran her hand along her cheek and tenderly brushed away the trails of dampness on her skin. "What do you say we get out of here?"

Penny nodded. "I didn't have time to get a hotel room. Do you think I could stay at your place tonight?"

Lauren laughed and touched her forehead to Penny's. "I think that would work for tonight but actually I was going to ask about coming to stay with you."

"With me?" Penny wrinkled her nose trying to work out what Lauren was talking about. "In Las Vegas?"

"Mmm-hmm." Lauren planted another tender kiss on Penny's lips before tipping her chin up with her fingers and locking her in her gaze. "I love you, Penelope Rothmoor, and I'll take any chance I can to be with you."

"I love you too." Penny's breathy response caused a flutter in Lauren's middle. "Las Vegas is a great place for taking chances."

"Come on. Let's go home and pack." Lauren intertwined their fingers and kissed Penny once more. Heat shot through her body at her lover's touch. She smiled mischievously as she led Penny out of the gallery. "At least let's go home. Maybe we'll save the packing for tomorrow."

Bella Books, Inc.

Women. Books. Even Better Together.

P.O. Box 10543
Tallahassee, FL 32302

Phone: 800-729-4992
www.bellabooks.com

7/20

CPSIA information can be obtained
at www.ICGtesting.com
Printed in the USA
LVHW042013141219
640521LV00001B/3/P

9 781642 471038